About the Author

Dianne Homan has been a dancer, teacher, vegetable gardener, off-grid cabin dweller, long-distance walker, as well as a writer. She has always felt a deep connection to the Earth. She is the author of "Walk Your Own Camino: Themes and Variations along the Camino de Santiago" and two children's books. As well, she co-edited two anthologies of northern writing – "Urban Coyote" and "Urban Coyote: New Territory." She lives outside Whitehorse in the Yukon Territory of northern Canada.

Mother Earth Legends: Eleven Stories for the Eleventh Hour

Dianne Homan

Mother Earth Legends: Eleven Stories for the Eleventh Hour

Olympia Publishers
London

www.olympiapublishers.com
OLYMPIA PAPERBACK EDITION

Copyright © Dianne Homan 2023

The right of Dianne Homan to be identified as author of this work has been asserted in accordance with sections 77 and 78 of the Copyright, Designs and Patents Act 1988.

All Rights Reserved

No reproduction, copy or transmission of this publication may be made without written permission.
No paragraph of this publication may be reproduced, copied or transmitted save with the written permission of the publisher, or in accordance with the provisions of the Copyright Act 1956 (as amended).

Any person who commits any unauthorised act in relation to this publication may be liable to criminal prosecution and civil claims for damage.

A CIP catalogue record for this title is available from the British Library.

ISBN: 978-1-80074-788-3

This is a work of fiction.
Names, characters, places and incidents originate from the writer's imagination. Any resemblance to actual persons, living or dead, is purely coincidental.

First Published in 2023

Olympia Publishers
Tallis House
2 Tallis Street
London
EC4Y 0AB

Printed in Great Britain

Dedication

To Greta, and all who act upon their love of Earth.

Acknowledgements

The story, M.E.L., previously appeared in "Tesseracts Seventeen: Speculating Canada from Coast to Coast to Coast." Gratitude to MaryAnn Annable for the book's subtitle. Many thanks to Marie Carr, Jerome Stueart, Patricia Robertson, and attendees of "A Walk Between Worlds" storytelling evenings who read, heard and gave feedback on stories in this collection.

MELIFLORA

In the days of the flat earth, pregnant women's bellies got wider and less contoured as the baby inside developed. Husbands would press ears against the flat plains of their wives' middles and intone the common benediction, "I see our baby's future, smooth as the far horizon."

Childbearing was easier then. Babies would only plump up once they'd started to nurse. The greatest sign of love a parent could show was to press a flat hand gently upon the child's breastbone, a reminder of prenatal innocence, of floating in the broad shallow lake of the womb.

Then Meliflora of the tender-eyed face and lean-muscled body, whom her husband loved to look upon, became pregnant and was glad at the absence of menstrual blood and the first small ripples of nausea. Her husband put his ear upon her belly even before it started to change and, believing that his emotion exceeded that of other husbands, wished to formulate a greater, more rousing, blessing to bestow. So he said, "I see our baby's future, as infinite as the dome of the sky."

Meliflora was awed by his creativity and touched by this daring expression of his love for her and their offspring. She kissed him deeply and wrapped her legs around him, and then she did it again, and then again.

Her husband wanted her to give up her job as Water Carrier for the duration of her pregnancy, but she convinced him otherwise. The shallow shimmering lake of their homeland would not contain water for much longer. In a few months, as happened every year, the lake would dry up and disappear, and it was only the filled jars of the Water Carriers that would sustain the people until the next rainy season. Every hand was needed, especially those that were young and strong. Besides, Meliflora let him know, the upright posture and swinging hips required for water transport were perfect antidotes to the discomforts of pregnancy. So he pressed his flat hand against her breastbone to express his innocent trust in her.

Within weeks though, Meliflora wondered if she was worthy of trust, or rather if her body was. Other women had started to notice and comment that the crests of her hip bones had failed, so far, to soften and flare open to allow for the belly's sideways expansion. The midwife had visited to press and massage but had departed clucking her tongue. Men who had gaped at her beauty with approval since her passage into womanhood now looked at her with skepticism. Her husband held her and teased her and told her all would be well. Again he placed his ear against her belly and uttered his blessing for their baby, because he knew it had pleased her so much the first time.

But her hips still failed to widen, and her belly started to bulge. Meliflora was concerned for the well-being of their child and disconcerted by the disapproval of the community. She draped long shawls over her shoulders to hide her roundness, pretending she'd come down with a chill. When she bent to pick up or put down a water jar, she turned sideways so others wouldn't notice that she had to splay her knees to get into a squat.

Meliflora's tender eyes took on a troubled look and, try as he might, her husband couldn't prevent his own expression from reflecting hers. When he leaned his head toward her belly, he didn't know where to place his ear. If he put it directly on top of the mound, he felt unbalanced and dizzy, if on the near side, his neck cricked and his view was blocked by her swelling. Then he couldn't see the babe's future at all.

He continued to go to the fields every morning as a caretaker of plants. He dipped his small ladle into the jar of water slung over his shoulder and trickled it over each of the vegetable plants in the portion of the plot for which he was responsible. He pulled the few weeds and left them to die in the dry dust that surrounded the specks of green he watered within the larger brown landscape.

But his work became affected by his troubles. He lacked confidence that he could support the life of his community if life within his own household was awry. His doubts sometimes made his hands shake. He was embarrassed in front of the other Caretakers. They sucked breath through their teeth when he spilled drops of precious water.

One day, Meliflora and her husband stopped going to work. A Caretaker of Community Members brought to their door, the usual provisions supplied in times of illness – a large jar of water, a deep basket of dried foods and sprigs of healing herbs. If the sick person, or persons, had not reappeared by the end of a month, then supplies for a comfortable death would be delivered by the same Caretaker.

When that good woman arrived at Meliflora's door with provisions the second time, she could tell no one was dying. Meliflora's face was rosier and more beautiful than ever. Her husband had funneled his nervousness and worry into caring for potted plants at each of their windows and going out at night to gather nuts and berries and to snare small game before the Gatherers of Wild Foods should do so at the start of their work day.

The caretaker surveyed the racks and bowls of food in their

home. "In all my years of being a Caretaker of Community Members, I have never seen anything like this," she said. "You have done the best for yourselves, but you have also done the worst." She referred to the punishment of banishment for those who do not contribute to the survival of the community and who break the food laws meant to provide for all.

Meliflora and her husband knew of this possible fate and cried before the woman to show their remorse. They begged her to leave with them the supplies for a comfortable death and promised that they would, in short order, turn themselves in to the Council of Elders for judgement.

"They will not be lenient, I fear," said the caretaker. She pointed at Meliflora's belly. "They are frightened by your grotesque shape. It negates all flat earth traditions." At that, she shoved her bundles toward them and fled the house hugging herself.

Meliflora and her husband turned to each other, placed trembling hands against breastbones rising and falling with quickened breath and, without a word, pulled out their sand sled and began to load it with potted plants, dried foods, water jars, the healing herbs they hadn't needed from the first delivery by the Caretaker, and the incense and ointments from the second delivery, just in case.

They set off after dark, not toward the distant lights of other communities but toward the horizon, the edge of the flat earth. All laws, all common sense, all old legends warned against ventures in this direction. Everyone said it was a wasteland of searing dryness and withering wind. Everyone said it held nothing but death. The Council of Elders would have banished them here, they were certain. But since they went of their own volition, they saw it as an act of courage and hope.

They soon enough discovered that nothing like bravery and spirit can survive for long in the hot arid winds near the edge of the world. They curled in on themselves like two desiccated leaves. Meliflora's round belly caught the gusts. At first she fought for balance and steadiness but quickly enough gave in to the reeling disorientation and staggered like a drunkard. Her husband pushed the sled with his head down and eyes closed. He feared he could not bear the sights that morning's light would bring – his potted plants flattened and brown, his wife's face creased with dust and exhaustion, the huge emptiness ahead, so close, so inevitable. He felt as though he were falling, waiting for impact.

What had they been thinking? That there would be an oasis? A cool shelter? An undiscovered shallow lake? They called themselves fools and carried on anyway.

They walked until they had to crawl. The blasts of wind grew so strong that movement in one direction was only possible in the manner of reptiles. At some point, Meliflora and her husband noticed they'd left the sled behind and didn't care. They could hear the edge of the earth ringing like a wet finger circling the rim of a water glass. Gasping with thirst, they crawled toward that vision with a sudden crazy hope for salvation.

But when at last they hung their heads over the outer limit of their world and saw dust flow in waves and swirl in eddies against the infinite dome of the under sky, Meliflora felt the need to vomit. She raised herself on hands and knees to heave, and the fierce wind reached under her belly and around her skirts and flung her off the edge.

Her husband, flat against the solid ground, grasped both her hands and looked wide-eyed into her tender face. She could read his lips when he tried to shout over the roaring gale, "I'll hold you forever."

The force of the dust and hot air pulled upon her, so her husband dug in his toes, working them farther back away from the precipice. Meliflora's arms, neck, torso and legs began to stretch with the constant pressures upon them. Her husband gripped her hands with all his might and inched his toes back, back, across the land, the stretch of his body matching hers.

His toes dug in and retraced their earlier steps across the howling desert, crossed through their own village where Water Carriers and Caretakers jumped out of the way, through the communities of distant lights, dug their way across planted fields and across dry beds of lakes. They scrambled and scrabbled through cracked clay and gravel and dust. And Meliflora's legs and feet hung so far below the disc of the earth that he could no longer see them.

Suddenly, his toes hit air, and he knew his feet had reached the opposite side of flat earth making it impossible to dig in any further. Meliflora saw his eyes widen in horror, saw him glance quickly backward over the land, the finiteness of which had deserted him. She looked under the earth in the same direction and saw his feet dangling over the far edge. They looked so helpless.

She felt a surge of strength then, through the lean and now incredibly long muscles of her young body. She swung her legs back then sailed them in a great arc forward until her feet went up and over her husband's, and her ankles locked over the backs of his.

And that's when everything changed. The edges of flat earth curved down with the pull of her weight until it was like an inverted bowl. Dust flowed down the slopes, covering the back of Meliflora's body and filling in the areas around her sides and limbs. The inhabitants of earth held onto trees and fence posts to keep themselves from being swept away.

Then Meliflora's rounded uterus contracted and her water broke. It cascaded into the space between her and her husband, washing the dry grime from their skin, replenishing the moisture they'd lost. Into the pool splashed one baby then another and another and many more. Meliflora and her husband laughed joyously and knew, with certainty, that all of the life and love they required was right there, in the blessed sphere contained by their joined hands and feet.

On the surface of the earth, people stood up, dazed, and discovered that up was still up and down was still down. They brushed off the dust and felt, somehow, brand new. The lakes filled with water from underground springs and the dry ground became loamy and fertile. The new hills formed by the backs of Meliflora's and her husband's bodies promoted the formation of rain clouds throughout the year and were clothed in carpets of wildflowers. The winds softened.

Later, when people grew brave enough to approach the former edge of the world, they found a previously unknown golden ore in the places where the fourth fingers of the hands of Meliflora and her husband were eternally intertwined. The Workers of Metals fashioned a symbol of love from the beautiful material, a circular adornment worn by those who pledge themselves to each other.

Forever after, on happy occasions like harvests, births and marriages, each person on this bountiful planet performed the most important symbolic gesture of all. They placed their hands flat upon the ground to give thanks, deep abiding thanks, to the round earth – the source of all life; the source of all love.

A PRAYER TO MELPOMENE

O Muse, I approach you now for the very first time, feeling nervous and tentative. Please forgive my awkwardness.

Until this theater season, I have called upon your sister Thalia, Muse of Comedy, and we danced well together. I wrote and staged light works that made audiences laugh, a pleasure for my ears. The actors cavorted, exaggerated, and gesticulated for the purpose of making exquisite fun of society and politics. As I see it, lampooning is a serious calling.

Now I feel called otherwise. Three things have brought me to you at this time, three things that make me wonder if I have been triply cursed by your immortal father, Zeus.

First of all, my only-too-mortal father died ten months ago. He was not ill, nor did he have a fatal accident. He was pruning his grape vines in the low winter sun, and he dropped to the earth as softly as one of his cuttings. A perfect death, one might say.

Yet I am troubled by more than his absence. You see, he attended my comedic plays and laughed and applauded. But afterward, in the taverna, he did not join the group around me, repeating the play's jokes or slapping my shoulder in congratulations. He turned instead to more sober conversation with his friends or to thoughtful study of a text at a corner table or to quiet reflection of the evening from his favorite spot on an outdoor bench. I never turned with him, filled as I was with the excitement of my own accomplishments. And so, I missed the opportunity to learn how to be a man like him.

Second, my dear younger sister has recently given birth to her first child and, instead of blossoming as new mothers usually do, she is deeply despondent. Neighbor women, shaking their heads, tell me this happens sometimes, but that doesn't comfort me. She sits by a window, unseeing of what is before her, oblivious to what is happening in the room behind her. So I pick up and hold my little nephew when he starts to fuss, and he is as rosy as a new day, as gurgly as living water, as wiggly as a playful pup. Later, after he drops off to sleep, I hold my sister, and it is like holding a fragile shell, one that could break under the slightest pressure. I sing her songs and repeat funny stories from our shared past, but still she does not smile.

Third, my best friend since childhood has gone off to war. My eyes seek him in vain in the local plaza. I cannot imagine him in a foreign setting, much less a place of constant danger. Whatever happened to his lighthearted ways? His face was so serious when he said that serving as a soldier was a necessary step toward manhood. He became angry when I questioned this assumption, so I bit my tongue. His departure has left me feeling deflated, leaky, as though a plug has been pulled from the base of my soul, and all the rich pleasures of friendship have spilled out, disappeared into the dust. I move with a dry rattling emptiness.

Melpomene, forlornly I sit at my writing table at the back of the theater and call upon you to help me make sense of everything. That is a huge request, I realize.

I have contemplated your image over the entrance to the theater many times in the past year. You are portrayed with the frowning mask of tragedy in one hand. Some say you bring sorrow, but I think they are mistaken. Now that my father is gone, my sister is in despair, and my friend is in danger, I see that sadness is like air. It is ubiquitous. We breathe it in. It is absorbed into our very blood. With your help, I may be able to move the heaviness of it from the hidden interior of my heart, perhaps of all hearts, to the public stage where it can be observed, where understanding can lead to catharsis.

No words come to me, though. I sit here without making one mark upon my parchment. What do you ask of me, Fair Muse? I realize that gods have expectations of us humans beyond simple prayers. Your sister, Thalia, sent the gift of written words to me once I had entertained her. I would put on the light slippers of a comedic actor and a costume piece suggesting a character, then let that fictional person use my body to come alive. My posture, tilt of the head, wave of the hands, manner of walking, expressions of surprise, nervousness, insult, sneakiness, and triumph were theirs. Only then would Thalia give me their words. I raced to pick up my pen, and my hand flew across the page, scarcely able to keep up with the inspiration she sent my way.

Shall I dress the part of a tragic actor? It is worth a try, although I fear this is where my awkwardness will become glaringly apparent. I sit on a bench by the costume room door to put on high, laced cothurni boots, with built-up soles thick enough to invite vertigo in the wearer. Tragedy is, after all, larger than life, and the actors must look the part. I drape a long cumbersome robe over my shoulders, an indication of the weightiness of the stories told in this, the most revered of art forms. I dare not put the tragic mask over my face for fear of losing all sense of balance and tumbling to the ground in what I imagine would be a rather comical manner. Instead I place it before me on a table, where it has a view of the performance space. I rise unsteadily and walk haltingly towards center stage.

There, in one instant, I feel your influence like a flash of lightning from the heavens – for that is where my head now finds itself. My vision becomes sharp and clear like an eagle's, and my thoughts fly close to your dwelling place on Mt. Olympus. I look down on the mortal world from above and experience a cool distancing, a longer and broader perspective.

"Oh Father," I cry out, for I feel him near me, revisiting the living plane of existence through my humble eyes and body, now elevated by a cleverly designed pair of boots. It becomes apparent to me, in this moment, that his turning at the taverna – to serious conversation, to reflection, to study – was not an indication of lack of appreciation for me and my art, but rather of a larger and more realistic view, not due in his case to tall stature, but attributable to the wisdom that comes with age. I narrow my eyes and see, from this great height, my work in the theater of comedy and my pride in achievement as small, temporary things. I turn toward the apparition of my father, and he holds out his hand to me. I reach out, expecting a manly handshake, but he clasps my right hand to his heart. Then he is gone.

I drop my head, and my eyesight is blurred for the duration of several shaky breaths. When it clears, I'm startled to see my feet stretching downward, toward a shadowy oblivion. From the thick solid soles of the cothurni boots, roots claw deep into the dark earth, all the way to the underworld, the Kingdom of Hades. From my viewpoint, still near Olympus, I can miraculously see details as small as a ripple in the river Styx and a single seed from an overripe pomegranate split open on the ground.

Suddenly I am hurtling downward, sucked through the roots, crying out in alarm. Then, all is still, and I stand on the river's shore, alone in the echoing gloom. Or have you accompanied me here, Melpomene? Are you guiding me toward another revelation?

I notice a wandering specter farther along the shoreline, but it is not you, O Muse. It is my sister, although I know her physical body, pale and weakened, is at home with her child. I see this gray aspect of her living self, peering up and down the river. Is she watching for the boatman? Is she eying the fruit of the pomegranate tree? I must intervene.

The cothurni boots enable me to approach in two mighty strides. This time when I hold her in my arms and sing her a song, she responds. "You've come to me here – all this way," she says.

"Return with me. Do not touch anything," I say, and hold out my right hand for her to grasp. I feel a healthy pulse and radiating warmth transmitted through her skin.

Then I am standing at the center of the stage once again and feel tears on my cheeks. Melpomene, I am awed by whatever just happened, so much so that I feel even more speechless than I did when first I approached you. The tragic mask observes me, silently, knowingly.

I feel you gently pressuring me onward. I am drawn back to the costume room where, in the properties chest, I come upon a silver dagger and a thyrsus wand, items with which you are often portrayed. You are a complex and mysterious deity, holding opposites in your hands. Is not a dagger a messenger of death? And is not the thyrsus wand, tipped with a pine cone and wrapped with a tendril of ivy, a symbol of life?

I pick up the knife in my right hand and the wand in my left and pace from one side of the stage to the other. My awkwardness has disappeared. The conduit of energy you opened in me, between the heights of Olympus and the depths of Hades, has been intersected now by a flow of power between right and left, death and life.

As I stride toward stage right, the knife, in a flash, stabs out, slashes the air. I am on a battlefield, protecting my friend. No enemies are able to approach. They retreat at the sight of me. At the edge of the platform, I turn and walk back to the left, the living components of the thyrsus wand before my eyes. I call for peace in our land and make signs of benediction with the prop I hold. Back and forth I pace, repeatedly marching into furious battle, then returning from war shouting demands for reconciliation, until I am utterly exhausted. When I can go no farther, I halt at the mid-point, breathing hard, heart pounding, and I nick the palm of my left hand with the tip of the knife. One drop of blood falls to the earth between my feet. I weep for a long time and do not question the reason for my tears.

Is that the late afternoon breeze picking up? Have I been here at the theater all day? I walk to the mask of tragedy on the table and look into its empty eyes, and beyond to a place of all-seeing. I put it over my face and my balance is steady and sure. I turn one time slowly, on the spot, and feel my father, my sister and my friend turning with me.

I then return the dagger, the wand, the mask, the robe, and the boots to their places in the costume room. I feel so small and light, yet more complete.

I sit once more at the writing table and roll the pen between my fingers. There is no sense of urgency, no feeling of worry. I hold up my right hand – the hand that vanquished my friend's enemies, that touched my father's heart, and that led my sister from the underworld. I am readying it for the next challenge – that of committing words to the page. I stretch it, twist it, shake it.

But then my left hand – the one that gave its blood, the one that held the wand of life – awakens, fumbles with the holding of a writing implement. Of its own accord, this clumsier hand messily scrawls the wondrous opening line of a new play. O Melpomene! What magic is this? I cannot begin to fathom your powers of inspiration. Full of wonder, I walk with you in spirit as I write, awkward and off-balance once again.

MELEKALUA

When Melekalua stands at the edge of the sea with a bright orange sunset in front of her and a blazing bonfire on the beach behind her, POOF, she turns into fire herself. Almost everyone on the island has seen this happen. It's not just me.

Lots of people have come to her for a healing at one time or another. We have doctors too, but there are things that doctors can't fix very well. So people ask my sister to help, and I help her. She says she couldn't do it without me.

I beat my drum – it's the first drum I ever made and has my favorite animal, a blue whale, painted on it – so she can journey to the spirit world deep in the ocean. There are other spirit worlds too, but she always travels to this one. Her power animal helpers give her advice or medicines or songs to bring back to heal the sick. And I keep drumming and drumming BOOM BOOM BOOM so she can find her way around that world and then to shore again. Sometimes my arms get so tired I think they will fall off, but I don't quit until I see her standing on the beach. And she's not even wet when she comes back, because the heat from her fire keeps her dry.

I made her shell rattle too. It's the best one I ever made. When there's a bonfire on the beach, and the person who's sick or sad is lying in the sand near it, she shakes and shakes that rattle CHUCKA CHUCKA. I drum and she rattles and we dance in a circle around the fire and around the person. Sometimes family and friends are there too. They have to dance and chant with us or Melekalua will ask them to go away. She says that if they're just being curious, or worse doubting, they will be like a heavy anchor and nothing will happen. It will all get dragged down.

So on those evenings, when everyone is in place and all is good to go, she nods at me to start drumming. We understand each other and I know her nod means 'good to go'. She shakes her rattle CHUCKA CHUCKA, the shell rattle I made for her, all around the person lying on the sand; and she sings a power song to the land and the water and the sky. The first part of her name, Mele, means song or chant, so Melekalua is a perfect name for her, and she says Polly is a perfect name for me because we live on an island that's part of Polynesia.

At first her shaking rattle sounds to me like the white edges of waves swooshing through gravel. Then when she dances her way toward the water, it sounds like clacking shellfish and raspy whale breaths. Finally the sound becomes crackly like fire and that's when WHOOSH, like a puff of smoke, she's gone. My eyes are usually closed to help me concentrate on keeping a steady beat and to keep my eyeballs from drying out so close to the fire. But I can see her POOF and WHOOSH anyway. It's as real as can be.

She is a good healer and she's a good sister. She does nice things for me. Three days ago, she made a birthday cake, and she always makes my favorite kind – white with blue frosting. Forty years, she said, from the day she and I washed up on this island. It was like being born, the way she tells it, splashing out from a watery place. I don't remember any of that. Melekalua says I cried and cried AIIEE AIIEE like a newborn. She's talked about a boat and an accident and our family being killed. My sister and I both have little scars on the tops of our heads under our hair, and they get itchy when we drum and rattle, from the vibrations

I guess. We laugh when we scratch our heads together. I also have a big scar across my forehead, and she says I was all bloody that day forty years ago. This story seems sad, but I can't find the feeling inside my body.

The old man who was shaman before Melekalua found us on the beach that day and knew what to do. He built a big fire and moved us closer little by little. He put a big butterfly bandage on my forehead to close up the cut. When my sister and I lay by the bonfire, she snuggled beside me, and when she put her arms around me, I looked down at our bodies and felt surprised. And then I breathed in a new way and stopped crying. Melekalua says she was eighteen and I was thirteen, and that was forty years ago, so we had birthday cake three days ago like we do every year on that date.

While we ate our two big pieces, she asked me what I can remember, and I said I remember the feeling of her arms around me. That was the most solid thing and also the most magical. I also remember the old man's eyes were the same color as the ocean. I remember his song sounded like gulls crying and his voice was up in the sky. And I remember that Melekalua suddenly sat up by that fire and started singing too, and that made me feel safe and I knew everything was going to be okay. Her song was like flutes and echoes WHOOEE WHOOEE and sounded familiar, like something I knew before we were born on the beach that day. It turns out my sister sat up and started singing because she was journeying with the old shaman. He was so surprised and happy, the ocean in his eyes sparkled.

He let us live in the little cabin behind his house and told us how he had come to the island in a boat to learn from the shaman before him, and the old man trained Melekalua to be a healer and taught me to make hand drums and rattles. The hand drums are easier to make than island drums, and that is important because I don't have nimble fingers. I thread the hides to the frames with thick sinew, and I paint them by aiming dots of color. My aim is good with a paintbrush when I decorate instruments, and with a drumstick when I drum.

And I aim well with a litter picker-upper, too. Every day after lunch, I clean up the beach and put bags of garbage in the dumpster by the road. It's crazy how much trash washes up – something about how the ocean currents flow around the islands. At the landfill, everything gets burned, and it's stinky because of all the plastic. Melekalua says it's too bad they can't burn it hotter, and then it wouldn't be so bad. But they have to throw it on a fire or the trash would be a mountain higher than Mauna Loa by now. Mauna Loa looks way down toward our beach on the sunset side of the island, and on the sunrise side is another peak called Kilauea, and those two mountains spit smoke and fire and sometimes lava flows all the way to the sea HISSS HISSS. Pele, the fire goddess, is supposed to live in Kilauea, and maybe I'm named after her, too, because I build the big bonfires on nights of healing ceremonies.

For forty years, I've lived in the little cabin on this island that's part of Polynesia below the volcano where Pele lives. I help my sister with healing ceremonies and with chores around the cabin and the shaman's old house that my sister moved into after the old man died. I clean up the beach. I make drums and rattles, and the ones that aren't for use at healings get sold in town. Tourists like them because I paint big sea creatures on the heads of the drums and little sea creatures on the handles of the rattles. When I'm in town with my sister, I watch the tourists pick up my drums and rattles, and they say nice things about them. But I don't think they know how powerful drums and rattles are. They never talk about the kind of journeying my sister does, they only talk about traveling here and traveling there on airplanes or boats. I figure if we were meant to travel, we'd have wings or fins.

I cleaned the beach today and gathered lots of driftwood for a fire, because Melekalua has someone coming this evening. It's Manny who was so cute when he was little, but now that he's a teenager, he scowls all the time. He reminds me of a mean dog going GRRR GRRR, but my sister says he's just trying to cover up his sadness.

Just before sunset, I have everything ready, because I know Melekalua counts on me. When the fire is big and looks like it's reaching for the sky, she walks with Manny and his parents and a few of his friends down onto the beach. She whispers something to the boy, and I know her whisper is good medicine because his scowling face smooths out and he lies on the warm sand near the fire. Melekalua nods at me and that means 'good to go', so I take my drum with the blue whale painted on it out of its bag and start to beat the rhythm she journeys to – BOOM BOOM BOOM. Then Melekalua's rattle, sounding like the white edge of the ocean swooshing through gravel, dances around Manny and she sings her power song to the land and sea and sky. We circle the fire, and the boy's family and friends are dancing and chanting, and I close my eyes, but I can still see. The sound of my sister's rattle gets deeper like clacking shellfish and raspy whale breath, then gets sharp like the crackle of fire and WHOOSH Melekalua is gone to the lower spirit world beneath the waves to ask for help for Manny.

I keep drumming and circling and Manny is twitchy, so I open my eyes part way so I don't step on him. And that's when I notice that his long sleeves have bunched up and there are cut marks on his arms and I think of the big scar on my forehead and whisper OUCH OUCH OUCH along with the drumbeat and it sounds like a power song that might help him, so I keep it going.

My arms get so tired they feel like they're going to fall off and the top of my head is itchy and I wish I could scratch. Melekalua has been gone a long time – longer than usual.

Suddenly Manny's eyes pop open and he gasps HYUH HYUH and sits up, and that's when I realize my sister is back on shore. But she is all wet and something is wrong.

Manny gets to her before anyone else has even moved. He's young and very fast, and he has a knife in his hand, and I don't know where that came from. Usually Melekalua would be dancing up the beach, shaking her rattle and singing, so my feet are stuck in their usual spot by the fire. But then I see that everyone else has run to her and that's when I set my drum on the dry sand and make my legs go down toward the water.

Manny's cutting away fishing line and six-pack rings and pieces of old netting that my sister is trapped in. I cover my eyes because the picture is a bad dream I think I've had before. I hear SHUFF SHUFF on the squeaky sand and open my eyes to see the others taking all that garbage to the fire and throwing it in. Manny is very carefully slicing a plastic bag away from her neck and mouth, and as soon as her mouth is uncovered she starts to sing a new healing song and Manny joins in, and that's when we all know something big has happened.

Manny's parents and friends and I come closer, and I can hear my heart going THUMP THUMP in my chest. Manny looks different as he and Melekalua sing together. His eyes are bright and he's not so pale, and he's not scowling. At the end of the song, she reaches for one of his hands and pushes his sleeve up and strokes the cut marks on that arm and says, "You came to help me in the spirit world." And he nods looking surprised.

I put my palms on my chest and push hard and whisper OUCH OUCH OUCH, and I turn and run, and my eyes are open but I don't see anything, and I just want to hide.

Next thing I know, it's morning and I'm all tangled up in my sheets and my long skirt, and as I twist and tug I see that my drum isn't in its place on the table, and I realize I left it on the beach and start to cry. I can feel the AIIEE AIIEE coming up in my throat.

And that's when my sister taps once on my door and walks in with two steaming mugs in one hand and my drum clutched between her elbow and ribs. I slap my hands over my eyes to push the tears back in.

"Here," Melekalua says. "Hot chocolate for you. With whipped cream on top, the way you like it."

Usually I reach for hot chocolate with whipped cream really fast, because I like how the liquid and the cream are two different temperatures at first, but I'm still pushing on my face. "Oh, Polly honey," she says.

I'm trying to get my throat to work so I can say something. My voice comes out all scratchy, "I was scared last night and I ran away." My hands start flapping.

She puts the mugs on the table and sits in the chair by the window and plays my drum softly. "Breathe and float. Breathe and float," she says. The palm trees waving in the wind outside the window make it look like she has seaweed hair, and I squint and blink. But then I look down, and I splutter like water went in my mouth and down the wrong pipe.

"But you said it was Manny who came to help you last night and not me." Then I really start to cry, and I'm yanking at my clothes and bedding to get free, and my face is getting hot.

Next thing I know, Melekalua's strong arms are under my

arms and around my back, and she's half-lifted me up and is swinging me side to side. She calls this the fish tail hula, and it's how she calms me down when I get really mad or anxious. It makes it so the bad feelings can just dribble out of my feet.

When she sets me back down on the edge of the bed, my skirt is straight and the sheets are on the floor, so I pick them up and dump them in the laundry basket by my headboard. She puts her hands on my shoulders and nods at me with one eyebrow up. I take a big breath. "Umm, good to go," I say.

She hands me my hot chocolate with whipped cream on top and it tastes really good. "You know I can't do it without you, right?" she says.

And I say, "I know."

She sips her coffee and nods and sips some more and nods some more, and I'm just about to say 'good to go' again when she says, "I'm really going to need your help a few days from now. It's the biggest healing ever."

"The biggest?"

"So big that I have to give Manny some training so he can help too." I stare into my cup and stick my lips way out. "A different kind of help than you give me, Polly. He couldn't do your part." I wipe my mouth and my eyes. This is a change and sometimes I have trouble with change, but I can tell my sister needs me, so I say okay.

"Do you have any drums made?" she asks, and I pull my case of frames and hides and sinew and paints out from under the bed and show her the drum I just finished lacing. "Good. Can you paint it in the next three days to be a special drum for Manny?"

I suck in breath and clamp my lips tight, and when she sees that she says, "Breathe and float, Polly."

The air comes out with a raspberry sound and that makes me

laugh even though I don't really think anything is funny.

"I know you can. Have you painted a swordfish before?"

I shake my head because I haven't done one before, but I stick out my tongue because I'm already picturing it in my mind.

"Good," she says again, and I love it when Melekalua tells me I'm good. I also love it when she does the fish tail hula with me and when she makes birthday cake or hot chocolate with whipped cream and when we drum and rattle together. She's a good sister.

She tells me that when Manny came to help her in the spirit world last night, he came as a swordfish. "You saw how fast he can move."

"Yes. And he has that knife, too."

"Exactly." Then she says she's off to Manny's, and she doesn't think she'll be home much in the next few days, and I tell her I'll be okay, but I miss her already and she's not even out the door yet.

She hugs me. "Things will get back to normal in three days." She pulls back and smiles and looks me in the eye, and her eyes look like the ocean. "If all goes well, it'll be the best normal in forty years."

"I like normal," I say and I wave and wave and wonder what she meant as she heads up the trail; and when I can't see her any more, I shrug and turn to my drum-making supply box.

I sit cross-legged on the floor and lay the just-finished drum on my lap. I stick my tongue out again so I can picture the swordfish, and my finger starts outlining its shape on the drumhead. Usually I draw and paint a sea creature in the center of the drum, but this time I'm imagining three swordfish swimming in a circle around the edge. That will show that they are fast. I check how much silver paint I have, because this is a very silvery fish. My finger is having fun following the curves of the bodies and the dorsal fins and the tail fins and the sword beaks that cut through the water. I rock from hip to hip to feel the swimming motion in my body, and then I'm ready to draw and paint. I make just a simple pencil outline, because my fingers don't work so well for details. But when I aim my paintbrush and my colors to fill in one of the swordfish and the ocean around it, it looks like a living thing has jumped right out of the water and landed on the drum.

So I rock and draw and aim and paint until that swordfish is done, and I realize I'm hungry and go to the kitchen in the house to get some leftovers from the fridge, and it's weird not to have my sister here at lunchtime. In the afternoon, like every day, I clean the beach. I put the full garbage bags in the dumpster by the road, and when I get home, Melekalua is still not there so I imagine her saying "Breathe and float" and remember that the biggest healing ever is coming up. I settle on the floor to outline the second swordfish.

For two-and-a-half days, I see my sister for just a few minutes before bedtime and at breakfast. She looks bigger than she usually does, and she laughs and says that the work of training Manny and planning for the big healing is filling her up. She whistles when she sees how the swordfish drum is coming along and says, "Good, Polly." And that feels really nice.

On the third day, the paint is all dry and the drum is finished and I've made a wrapped stick and a cloth bag to go with it. I go to the beach in the afternoon and make sure it's extra clean and I gather lots of driftwood at the bonfire site and I'm excited and a little scared because I don't know what a big healing will be like.

I bring Manny's new drum and my drum to the beach just before sunset and start the fire, and right away something's strange because a big flatbed truck backs onto the beach, right down to the high tide line, and I'm mad and want to yell at the driver to go away, but then I see that Manny's dad is the driver and he waves at me. OOF OOF goes my breath as if I've been hit in the stomach and I turn my back to him and his truck because I don't know what it all means. Melekalua and Manny are walking down to the sand, and I hardly recognize Manny because he looks grown up and strong.

My sister asks me to give the swordfish drum to Manny so I do, and he takes it out of the bag and his eyes get big and he runs his hand over the three silver creatures as if they're good friends and then he looks at me and says, "Thank you, Polly," and I can tell he's happy.

Melekalua has her rattle out and looks ready to start, but I'm confused because there's no sick person lying on the sand. Then she looks at each of us, including Manny's dad in the truck, and says, "We are doing a healing tonight for the spirit world. I couldn't do it without the three of you and my power animal helpers. This will take longer than other healings, and we'll all get so tired we'll want to stop. But we cannot stop until it's finished." She puts an arm around my shoulders and whispers, "Polly, you'll have to drum for a long time, and I know it will feel as though your arms are falling off. But whatever happens, even if something scares you, keep beating your wonderful blue whale drum."

OOF OOF goes my breath again, because I'm nervous, but I nod 'good to go' because I know my sister needs me. And then she shakes her rattle, and it's like all the palm trees and the stars and the tops of waves wake up. I feel the hair on my arms stand up. She sings her song to the land and sea and sky. Then I start the beat and Manny joins in, and the two drums beating together sound like huge waves pounding on the shore. I dance around the fire with my eyes closed and, even so, I can see Manny's dad beating the rhythm on his steering wheel and Manny moving fast, darting this way and that like a swordfish, and Melekalua dances toward the shore and WHOOSH disappears.

Manny starts to sing a song I haven't heard before and, since his voice is deeper and louder than my sister's, it sounds like it could cut right through the water to reach the bottom of the sea. Then he puts his drum in its bag and sets it on a patch of clean dry sand before he moves toward the shoreline, and I think maybe he'll POOF and WHOOSH away too.

But he doesn't, and just then a tall wave approaches, and I run to the high side of the fire and want to yell to Manny and his father to watch out, but I can't make a sound and it takes all of my concentration to keep beating my drum like my sister told me. So I stare at the blue whale painted on my drum, and I think it nods at me. My mouth pops open, and I think a yell is going to come out, but the sound is more like another power song and my drumming arm gets a boost of energy, and it's a good thing, because that one big wave splashes Melekalua and an enormous blue whale up, up out of the deep and onto the flatbed of the truck, and my sister has one hand on the whale's side and the other is shaking her rattle hard, and she looks even bigger than she has the last few days, and her face is working hard as she chants. I can't tell if she's wet from seawater or from sweat.

Manny waves to his dad and VROOM the truck starts up the beach, and that's when I see that the whale's fins and tail are all tangled in plastic, and that plastic is tangled in more plastic and more plastic, so as the truck goes up the beach and turns onto the road, there is a long wide trail of garbage being towed behind.

And now Manny has his knife out, and I see his swordfish

speed as he slashes at fishing line and six-pack rings and old nets to free any sea creatures that are trapped so they can flop back into the water and swim away, and his knife is moving so fast I only see flashes of reflected firelight here and there and here and there.

And I drum and drum, and my dance feels like the movements of the sea creatures getting loose and swimming away, and it's the best dance ever. Except that I don't know when it will end, and that makes me nervous again.

The trail of plastic is like a river that is flowing and flowing and Manny keeps cutting and cutting and I keep drumming and drumming, and my arms are getting tired but of course I don't stop. I close my eyes so I can see, and there is Manny's father driving east on Route Eleven, the road that goes right by the rim of Kilauea, and I wonder if my sister will ask for help from the fire goddess Pele, whose name is like mine, but her fire in the volcano is much hotter than any fire that I could ever build. And I see that truck going up the road and it's not travelling fast because it's pulling all that garbage behind so it'll take quite a while to get there, and that's how long Manny and I will have to do our jobs here on the beach, and he's sweating and I'm sweating. But he nods at me and I nod at him; and he sings his song; and I open my mouth and let whatever-it-is come out and do my freedom dance, and sparks fly out of the top of the bonfire up to the stars.

That river of plastic keeps moving by me – on and on and on – and all of a sudden I understand how big a healing this is, and maybe it's my eyes playing tricks on me but the ocean seems sparkly like the old shaman's eyes when Melekalua first sang with him. Manny is sparkly too with sweat and seawater and fish scales and flashing knife blade, and my eyes get dry and sore and

I close them again.

And I see the truck approaching the overlook area above Kilauea's crater and the whole scene glows orange, and Manny's dad backs the flatbed right up against the fence. And even though my arms feel like they're about to fall off, I beat my drum with all my strength so it will help my sister up on the slope of Mauna Loa. And maybe she hears it, because I see her look back down the mountain towards our beach and nod. Then she puts her hand higher on the whale's body, and it looks like she's as big as it is now. She shakes her rattle above both of their heads, and the whale spouts a huge rush of water over the two of them, then WHOOSH POOF they're swept off the truck and away, riding on top of the river of lava down to the ocean.

Then I scream, partly because of what I've seen with my eyes closed and partly because of what I see with my eyes open. The river of plastic is a flash flood and it's moving so wild and fast I'm afraid it could pull me in. I stumble around the fire away from it and try to find Manny. And there he is in the middle of the river with his knife moving like lightning, and the garbage races up the beach on each side of him and fish and turtles and crabs flop back into the water at his feet. And I'm filling up and getting bigger from so much drumming and the top of my head itches terribly and still I think I'm screaming, but maybe it's the sound of tons of plastic scraping across the sand SCREE SCREE and along the road and up the mountain and into the fire of Kilauea where Pele is opening her mouth and swallowing every last bit. And then it all stops.

Nothing more is coming out of the ocean. Manny turns to look at me. I drop my drum and my arms fall off. I'm so swollen that my clothes are strangling me, and Manny runs to me with his knife and cuts them away. He pushes me toward the water then puts his hand on my head. He brushes away loose hair and the itchy scar opens up and I breathe through it. He backs away and picks up my blue whale drum and plays it, and I know he's playing it just for me. I wriggle and squirm my way beyond the breaking waves and soon I'm surrounded by the sounds of the deep, and I hear Melekalua calling to me WHOOEE WHOOEE from under the water. I aim myself in her direction, and my flukes beat a rhythm like a shaman's drum.

MELISSA

Melissa Melligan (her real name) auditioned for the part of Mother Nature in the margarine commercial. She knew she was perfect for it because, as she kept reassuring herself, she had the blue eyes of a clear sky and wavy hair like the sea. She was tall and statuesque like a high mountain. She moved with the grace of wind-blown grass. She chided herself for getting carried away with such clichéd metaphors. But in her heart, she knew she truly was Mother Nature – or at the very least, one of her cells or nerve-endings.

Apparently, the casting agents agreed with this assessment, because they hired her on the spot after one take. As the cameras rolled, she chewed a bit of the slathered bread and could tell it wasn't butter. But she made it appear she was in gustatory heaven.

And the climactic moment, when she said, "It's not nice to fool Mother Nature," throwing wide her arms, a movement that would, during filming, cue the special effects guys to create the lightning and thunder, well, it literally blew her audience of judges away. They said they could feel electricity in the air. The costumer was called in right away to measure her for a diaphanous blue gown, silver slippers, and a crown of flowers.

That evening, Melissa called her mom and then Tara, her best friend since childhood. Both were absolutely tickled to hear the news of her successful audition. When Melissa said, "Mother Nature is so real to me," her mother said, "I've seen that in you since you were born."

Tara's response to the same comment was, "For sure! And I really want to try on your costume."

When they were kids, Mellissa and Tara played in the woods behind their houses every day, rain or shine. They dressed up in anything silky and flowing and pretended to be wood nymphs or flower fairies or water sprites. They made themselves wands, and everything they touched became magic – wood would speak, flowers would dance, water would sing soothing tunes.

As they got older, rather than hanging out at the drugstore with boys or going window shopping, they graduated to being Sister Earth and Sister Nature, daughters of the mothers with the same last names. In these roles, they picked up litter, set up bird baths in both their yards, wrote letters to congressmen they weren't old enough to vote for to express their environmental concerns, and got into organic gardening. And they hadn't left the magic behind. During their hikes in the forest, they talked to animals and tried to affect the weather.

Melissa never said anything to her friend, but Tara was no good at the supernatural stuff. Tara would whisper, "I'm going to invite that chipmunk to come to me," then she'd hold out her fingers as though she had a bit of food held there and make kissy noises. It was embarrassing. Melissa sat just behind her friend and either sent an ESP message to the chipmunk if she could see its eyes, or she'd wiggle her nose. The actress on *Bewitched* did that move years after Melissa had perfected it. The TV show made it seem corny, but for her it had really worked. The chipmunk came closer until Tara scared it away by yelling, "I did it! I did it!"

When it was a nasty rainy day, Tara would stand on the porch with her face turned upward and chant in a spooky voice, "Rain,

rain, go away. Come again some other day." Melissa would just breathe deeply, imagining her exhalations pushing the clouds away. Next thing they knew, they were running under rainbows seeking out pots of gold sunshine.

After high school, Tara got a job in a garden center, and Melissa went to acting school out west. She missed the nature girl part of herself, living in the city and spending so much time with humans instead of trees and animals. That's why she got so excited when she heard about the margarine commercial.

During her next phone call home, she invited Tara to come visit for a week. Her friend could watch the filming and, yes, at a free moment in the dressing room, try on the Mother Nature costume.

Melissa took the city bus to meet Tara at the airport. They hadn't seen each other since Tara's wedding a year and a half earlier. Melissa felt a little guilty that she hadn't been at her best for that event after two days on the Greyhound. This visit would more than make up for it. Tara would see her on her new, palm-tree-enhanced home turf, watch her in action on a professional television set, and hear all the things she'd been up to, which were totally different and so much more interesting than anything that anyone could be doing in their boring home town.

She only had to wait at carousel twenty-seven in the baggage claim area for a few minutes before she spotted Tara coming toward her, looking radiant. Her hair was so shiny, her cheeks so pink, her eyes so bright. Melissa opened her arms and projected her voice through the crowd. "Tara!" she called, and the two old friends hugged and laughed and looked at each other's faces.

"You look fabulous!" they said at the same time, and they hugged and laughed some more.

Both realized they were starving, so they walked arm in arm

toward one of the airport restaurants. Melissa said she'd get them a table while Tara made a pit stop. As she entered the eatery, she asked for two glasses of champagne to be brought to the table with the menus.

A minute later, Tara was bustling over to sit opposite her friend, saying, "I can't wait to tell you all the news," and because Melissa had expected to hear, "I can't wait to hear all your news," she froze, just as inexperienced actors tend to do when they forget a line. Thank goodness that's when the champagne showed up, and Melissa improvised like the pro she was and lifted her glass to Tara.

"To friends," she said. Tara raised her glass and repeated the toast heartily. But then she set the drink back down and pushed it an inch away.

"I'm pregnant," she said, then again with a squeal, "I'm pregnant!" Melissa reached across the table for her hand, and Tara bubbled, "Isn't it great?" Melissa tried hard not to crush her friend's fingers.

Tara talked non-stop through the meal and the bus ride to Melissa's place about how sweet and caring her husband Sam was, and how he had such a good job that it was no problem to fly out here for a week's visit, and how she'd seen Melissa's mom in the grocery last week and she'd guessed right away that Tara was pregnant and promised not to spill the beans to Melissa, and how being pregnant felt so spiritual, like having a Garden of Eden inside. *Yackity yack, yackity yack*, thought Melissa.

They had four days until the commercial would be filmed. They went for walks and hung out on the beach, and Tara said she wouldn't mind going shopping for some fashionable maternity clothes. Melissa stayed focused by practicing her part in front of the bathroom mirror before and after her shower each day. She studied her facial expressions, the inclination of her head, the careful, but natural-looking, shaping of each word in her line. But she couldn't do the full arm movements to show Mother Nature's wrath without knocking aspirin and make-up and mouthwash off the shelf, not to mention ripping down the droopy plastic shower curtain. So she did the actions in miniature accompanied by an outbreath suitable for a deadly karate chop.

On the big day, she and Tara got off the bus outside the studio. There was no celebratory bottle of champagne in Melissa's bag, but she was excited anyway. Tara was asking lots of questions and saying how amazing it would be to see her best friend on television. "This is just like when we were kids playing in the woods, only a hundred times better," she said, and Melissa hugged her.

Tara found various places to sit, out of the way, while Melissa was prepped by hair, make-up, and costumers, then while she received final notes from the director on the set. Melissa breathed, channeling earth energy through every pore, and indicated she was ready.

When the director called, "Action," she was the veritable embodiment of Mother Nature. She tasted the slathered bread, she realized she'd been duped, she said her big line, then threw her arms authoritatively, majestically, wildly, just as she'd imagined during her bathroom practice sessions. The thunder sounded, and the lightning flashed. Wow, that was amazing, she thought.

But no one was looking at her. They were shouting and swearing at the blackened, smoking bulbs in the stage light fixtures that had been so carefully focused on her. Some of the crew were running off to get new fuses and electrical tape to fix the blown sound equipment. Others were heaving the fake trees back up on their weighted bases.

The director skittered in all directions, then suddenly was at her side. "Honey," he said, "you were great. But we're gonna have to run that again. The ending didn't take – scorch marks all over the film. I'll have to give the power company what for. Must have been one helluva surge."

Melissa knew it had nothing to do with the power company. So on the second run-through, she toned down the arm fling. The director watched the take and shook his head. "Sorry, Hon," he said. "We'll need to do it one more time. That one was kinda flat. You gotta give it more oomph."

Melissa glanced at Tara, who nodded encouragingly to her. She took her place and tried to think positive thoughts. "Third time's a charm," she whispered to herself.

When the director called, "Action," she composed her face and body as befitted her role.

Once again, she tasted; she realized; she growled, "It's not nice to fool Mother Nature." And she let it rip.

There was smoke everywhere, and the crew lay sprawled on the floor. The director's eyes were wide and white in a blackened face. "Let's take a break," he sighed, "until we can clear this up."

Melissa headed to the door, cocking her head to Tara. "Dressing room," she said. As soon as they'd closed the door behind them, Tara started cooing and rubbing Melissa's shoulders. Melissa shrugged her off and unpinned the halo of flowers from her hair. "This would be a great time for you to try on the costume, if you're still interested," she said.

A slow grin came over Tara's face, and she touched the soft fabric. "You bet I'm still interested." So Melissa slipped off the gown and slippers as Tara removed her blouse and jeans and sandals. Melissa threw on her street clothes.

"I'll be back in a few minutes. Have fun," she said. At her friend's questioning look, she added, "Umm, going out for a smoke." And swept theatrically out the door, hearing Tara stutter, "B-but you don't..."

Melissa let herself through the fire door into the alley where the dumpsters stood. She thumped the heel of her hand against the metal side of one, and it made a deep echoing rumble. "There's your damn thunder," she yelled.

There had been a brief afternoon shower while all the craziness had been going on inside. She took a huge breath, the kind that actors are taught to calm themselves, and registered just how much she loved the smell of rain on warm pavement. Three butterflies landed and flexed their colors at the shimmering edge of a puddle. She heard birds and looked up to see swallows swooping under the eaves of the building opposite. A gray rat scuttled from beneath one of the dumpsters. It stopped in the middle of the alley, turned toward her, and opened its pink mouth. Melissa heard, "This is what's real."

"You do ESP!" she exclaimed as the rodent scurried away around a corner. Then she nodded to herself, taking in the rat's message. She was Mother Nature. For real. Just like the birds and the puddles and the butterflies and the rat. What was inside the film studio, in front of a painted set, with manufactured sound effects was pretend. She just had to perform it that way – as imaginary child's play, as a game.

When she got back to her dressing room, it was empty – no Tara, no costume. She figured the gown must have been taken for cleaning, and Tara probably tagged along. But there was no sign of anyone in the costume shop either.

She arrived at the studio door just in time to see Tara, stately and stunning in the blue gown, fling out her arms, see the crew members flick the switches that completed the circuits for the lightning and thunder, and hear the director crow, "Cut! That's a wrap!"

Tara looked as shocked as Melissa felt. "I was just standing in for a lighting and sound check," she said.

"You were brilliant! Brilliant!" said the director. "Let me get your name down here. Is that spelled T-E-R-R-A?"

Tara cut her visit short and went to the airport later that afternoon. Her old friend's laughter was freaking her out. Every time Melissa said, "Really, it's okay," Tara screeched back, "How could it possibly be okay?"

Melissa used the months until the lease on her apartment ran out to take kayaking classes at the pool as well as Wilderness First Aid and River Rescue through the local Red Cross chapter. She joined the Sierra Club and took part in canoeing, rafting and hiking trips. Everyone said she was a natural.

She moved to a small town in the mountains where a lot of back-to-nature types lived. She got a job with a wilderness tourism operator and, just for fun in the off-season, did some community theater in the local school gym. Within a few short years, she'd gained quite a reputation as a guide. Customers requested her. Word had gotten out that, on her trips, the wildlife viewing was as good as guaranteed. And somehow the weather was always perfect, as if someone were blowing the clouds away. Melissa just had to remind herself, when pointing out an animal, an important historical site, or a notable feature of the landscape, not to move her arms too fast.

MELCHIOR

The tug of the divine pulls us slightly north of westward, farther and farther from my home. My fellow students of astrology, Caspar and Balthazar, and I, Melchior, recognize its presence nightly in the bright star prophesied so long ago. We three have this in common – that ever since we were young children, we have thrilled to the patterns and stories of the night sky and have always hoped this foretold beacon would appear during our lifetimes.

I realize our lifetimes are inconsequential when compared with the vastness of the celestial realm. My father, who is also our teacher, reminds us of this whenever any of us complains about, or is distracted by, everyday occurrences. He points up at the clear night sky and has us ponder the infinite gifts we receive from above, like kisses from angelic beings. We reflect on his words and know ourselves to be wiser for them. As we learn the history, the mathematics, and the legends of the skies, it seems that we dwell on a plane that lies suspended between the Arabian sands and the stars on high, solid as the earth in body, yet with souls able to fly.

And now fly we do, as fast as our camels can carry us, for the glorious star has given us a sign that a new king, a messiah, a savior has come. My friends and I must travel and see for ourselves.

Caspar hails from a northern land of rugged mountains, and Balthazar is from a kingdom near the sea to the south. They came last year to learn from my father, our teacher. Naturally, I have been his pupil since I first learned language, and have seen many students from many lands come and go. Finally, I have reached the age of the typical apprentice. Caspar and Balthazar are the first to be my age-mates and, therefore, the first I have also considered friends – and a good thing too, as, on this journey, we are tested daily in many ways and must rely on each other.

Our teacher stayed behind not only because he feared his age would slow us down, but because, as a man devoted to objective studies, he knows that observations of the sky are best understood from more than one vantage point. I refer to him more often as "our teacher" than "my father". His students through the years, myself included, have addressed him as Sir, and he treats all of us the same as we eat and sleep and learn under his roof.

He was already a well-respected, gray-haired teacher of astrology when I was born, and decades older than his wife. She, my mother, died within days of my birth, and that is all I know. My father has taken adequate care of me but perhaps has never forgiven me for her death. He is open and giving and passionate when sharing his knowledge of the stars, hence my attachment to him as teacher. As a father, he is a stranger.

Of late, he, Caspar, Balthazar, and I spent entire nights lying among the dunes, away from the moist, obscuring air of the oasis. Our excitement mounted when we first observed an extraordinary series of stellar coincidences. In the course of my studies, I've learned that there are five heavenly bodies, some of the brightest, which behave like no others in their journey across the zodiac. Occasionally, each of these five mysteriously slows, halts for a time, reverses direction, slows again, and finally resumes its east-to-west pathway. When first I saw this happen as a boy, I felt great fear. What powerful being could disrupt the motion of a star? Our teacher responded by insisting that I, his student, see the larger patterns, ones that young men may be prone to miss or dismiss. He was correct, for when I considered my observations over spans of years rather than spans of days or weeks, the small discrepancies fit themselves into bigger pictures. Similarly, a few runaway camels do not alter the great trade routes across the desert.

But the coincidences of late have been as frankly astounding as would be a ship sailing across the sands of Arabia. The three largest of the bright wanderers have slowed to initiate a turn, two to commence their retrograde paths and one to retrace its route, at the very same time. And not only are they in close proximity to each other but also to the large star the Romans call Regulus, meaning "the king", seen in the constellation of the lion. We tremble to consider that we lowly students might be among the very few to have noted and understood this stellar phenomenon as the message that has been awaited by devout believers for centuries.

Some in our settlement by the oasis, regarding the brightening patch of night sky, expressed fear that it signals an end, a burning up, a cleansing fire sent by God to finish the work of his great flood. There was much keening and wailing. My friends and I would not have been able to sleep much anyway, due to keen anticipation of our expedition to follow the beacon. But as we travel now through unpopulated country, I thank the stars for their silence.

But are they silent? When the wind is still, I seem to hear a faint arpeggio, as though the glimmering lights from above travel toward our eyes on long silvery strings that stroke their neighbors in passing. In this way, starlight is like music playing itself.

Our teacher would look at me askance were I to say this in

his presence. He'd suggest my mind is playing tricks on me. I admit I have not slept well or enough since we set out. I am the untraveled one of us three and therefore the most unsure and nervous. Caspar and Balthazar try to cheer me with jokes and light conversation. They often remind me how lucky I am to have grown up in dry climes where the stars seem so close, so reachable. At this point though, I wish they would speak no more of stars.

Night after night, we slavishly follow this looming giant, and, rather than inspiring confidence in me, it is contributing to my malaise. By narrowing my attention to one blinding source of light, I have lost my bearings. I cannot orient myself to the larger map of the sky. And when the breeze picks up, the biting sands shift and swirl beneath us. Then I lose, as well, all sense of groundedness in the land of my forebears and feel as orphaned as I must have when a helpless new-born child.

And how long will this mystery star guide us? Will it abandon us in a strange place? I become unreasonably angry imagining that the heavens may be playing a dangerous trick on us.

Caspar hands me some dried meat, and from Balthazar I receive choice pieces of fruit. The first bite makes me cough and gag. One of them suggests we stop and make tea. We have never before, during this quest, taken a break during the night, but both of them quietly insist they need a short rest, too. As they start a small fire with desiccated dung and portion out the water, tea leaves and sugar, I stretch my stiff body upon the sand. Maybe I drift off, just for a few minutes. In that brief time, the hours-long swaying motion of my camel becomes the rocking of the earth beneath my back, and then becomes the comforting back-and-forth of a mother's arms. I wake to the smell of tea with a tear in the corner of each eye. My friends speak softly, as we sip our tea, about all we have shared during the year of our acquaintance – the teachings, the stories, the truths of young men's hearts and minds, the significance of our undertaking.

My strength and spirit revived by their kindnesses, we continue through the night until the star is lost in morning's light. We have traveled far enough now that we are in a more populous land. Being a child of the wide sands, I never imagined so many roadways, so many towns. Caspar and Balthazar are worldlier than I and take the lead in approaching strangers for information. What is being said about the star? Is there any word about the appearance of a new-born king? Who are the local astrologers and sages who might direct us onward? A few helpful words, a few pointed fingers have quickened our pace. We follow a road for part of the day until we feel we must sleep for at least a few hours. We hope that when we awaken at sunset, the star will show the way to our goal.

That night, we skirt the northern shore of the Dead Sea, and the star is reflected in its waters. It appears that no one can sleep for the brightness, and many are out of doors, gossiping, speculating, spreading rumors. Some point at us and refer to us as kings from the East. We humble students, kings? It is laughable. But we study each other and realize that, perched high upon our noble-headed camels, wrapped in our well-made winter cloaks, and wearing the head-dresses of our cultures, we do perhaps look exotic enough to be royal. We sit taller on our mounts.

Some whom we pass suggest we make our way to Jerusalem to greet Herod, the King, but we doubt we could pull off the charade. We bypass the city, and the star throbs like a happy heart. "Just ahead," it seems to say.

We nap one last time through an afternoon, rise near sunset, eat and wash ourselves at a village well. Now we are all three nervous, questioning our sanity, realizing we have no idea what lies in store. There could be well-equipped armies, locked gates, guards who must be bribed, or impenetrable crowds. Why had we never considered the possibility of failure?

We've been following roads, but now, as evening darkens to the color of royal purple silk, the star pulses and a ray of golden light descends directly to a point across a grassy plain. Does that make sense, we wonder? Wouldn't a gift from God, a new king, be found right along a well-traveled route? The star pulses again, and we lose the ability to doubt. We steer our camels off the road and toward the bright spot.

The field is not empty. There are two shepherds with their flocks, walking in the same direction we are. Ah, the crowds must be ahead, I think. And there. There is a structure with the glow of lanterns from within. In a moment we will see the guards, the armies.

But there are no crowds, no armies, no guards. And the structure is nothing more than a stable, a place for animals to take shelter. I think again that the heavens have tricked us. My companions' faces show the consternation I feel. But just then, we move into the warm light from a window, and my friends look, even to me, like splendid nobles of the East. I take the lead for the first time in our journey and motion that we should dismount.

The shepherds reach the door just ahead of us and peek inside. We hear from within a warm voice saying, "A humble welcome to this humble space." We all enter, and the shepherds stand to each side of the doorway.

My mind and heart become quieter than they've been since

before the joined star appeared. Its bright light is blocked, at the moment, by the beamed ceiling, the hayloft and the solid roof overhead. And yet, there is an emanation. The three of us approach. In the center of the room is a manger filled with straw, and a baby lies within – a boy child. The father, a slightly graying and hugely smiling man, and the young and fair mother sit close together on a rough-hewn bench. The emanation is the love that shines in the eyes of this small family.

The father rises to greet us. "Ah," he says, "here we have a few men with the kind of wisdom necessary to follow a star – a star which seems to promise so much, don't you agree? Yet, as you can see, all of the promise is held within this one small child." He strokes the baby's cheek. "It is a miracle," he whispers.

"Is this the king?" I ask, and the mother laughs with delight.

"To me, he is the king of kings," she says. "But I can imagine every mother saying that about her first-born son." She gently regards the three of us. "I am sure your mothers felt this way about you, as well, when you were born."

I clasp my hands to my chest and bow my head. I can hardly breathe with the wonder of the gift I have just received. I fall on my knees, and Caspar and Balthazar, looking dazed, lower themselves as well. Yes, it is proper to kneel before a king, I think.

Oh, but it is also proper protocol to bring gifts to a king, and we have nothing to offer. "Please forgive us," I beg. "We are but students and have just made this mad hurried journey and have committed the gravest of errors. We should have brought offerings fit for a king, no matter how small he is."

The parents are shaking their heads, but then Caspar speaks as though just awakening. "A gift," he mumbles. "Like gold?"

He reaches into his traveling pouch and the pocket of his robe, looking perplexed as though there should be nuggets there. Then a bit of mischief sparks in his eye.

He hastens to the door and stretches his arms out into the night. His upturned palms are suddenly ablaze with yellow starlight. "Gold!" he proclaims, then claps his hands together, rushes back to the manger, opens his hands, palms down, and shakes them over the child. The little one laughs and kicks his legs, and we can't help laughing, too.

Then Balthazar announces that myrrh, the most precious of oils, is a fine gift for a king. He rubs his hands together then lifts the loosened end of the blanket to apply imaginary oil to the boy's feet. He sighs and gurgles, and we echo his pleasure.

It is my turn, and my mind goes blank. What do I know about royal custom? Nothing. Then I recall a detail from a story told to me by one of my father's East African students. It had to do with frankincense. "There is a special resin from a tree that grows far from here," I say. "The spirit of the tree rises from deep underground where the waters of life dwell. The wondrous sap is offered by the tree to humans, and when we burn it, the fragrant smoke carries our prayers all the way to heaven." And I put my hands together, lift my face, and say, "Thank you, God." I fear that, perhaps, I have just babbled nonsense and feel my face flush. But when I glance at the others, the parents of the little babe are looking at me with gratitude. They hold hands with each other and extend their other hands to us. We, in turn, clasp ahold and reach out to the shepherds who join us. Around the child is a circle of love, and wordless blessings flow.

We sleep that night in the stable with the family. What luxury to close our eyes in the dark. The music of the stars is a lullaby that carries us to a place of pure peace.

At first light, the three of us depart after kissing the forehead of the baby and bowing over the hands of the parents. We ride east, each of us lost in our own thoughts. I wonder if Caspar and Balthazar are, like me, still relishing the image of being held by our mothers, being considered a king of kings, being loved so well. Hours later, when the sun goes down behind us, we turn to look at the star and see that the three wandering lights have departed from Regulus, the king. Two are now commencing their retrograde paths, and the third is retracing its earlier steps.

Then, so do we three wanderers separate, still clearly following celestial guidance. Caspar and Balthazar suddenly desire, above all else, to travel directly to their homelands, there to share the wonders of what we have seen and learned. And I am the one retracing my steps across the desert, unafraid to journey alone now, surely and steadily balanced between the solidity of land and the soul of stars.

The sun enters the constellation of the water-bearer as I make my way home, and as is usual for the season, the rains come. Many years, they tend to tease or torment, but this time they are gentle and steady. I raise my face to the sky and feel myself baptized by the firmament above, feel my thirsty roots sink deep into the earth. And around the moving feet of my camel, all the colors of creation suddenly sprout forth, bloom wildly, and release seeds to the care of the wind – the marvel of new life as far as the eye can see.

So much beauty fills my heart to overflowing, just as the beauty of the child's mother did in the stable near Bethlehem. It is only then that I realize I do not know the names of the child, the mother, and the father. I have been given a life-changing vision, yet lack the necessary words with which to speak of it clearly and accurately. I could kick myself. Yet the baby communicated without words by laughing, gurgling, and meeting our eyes. There is much to be learned from this example.

I ride into the settlement around the oasis, and all is calm. No more talk of fire and flood, no more wailing with fear. I wonder – has everyone forgotten the star? I tell myself to hold on to the miraculous, to resist the gravity of the ordinary.

At the door to the house in which I've lived my whole life, I feel strangely shy upon entering. The teacher is asleep in his chair by the window. He must have watched the stars for many hours last night. I sit across from him and am about to say "Sir." Instead I say, "Father." His forehead creases, then smooths. His eyes open, and I take in the fact that they are the same color and shape and size as my own. My breath catches with the pleasure of this discovery.

Then, from my lips, unpremeditated, comes the question, "What was my mother's name?"

The old man blinks rapidly, and again his forehead tightens. When it finally relaxes, he looks for a long minute at me, seeing, I think, a changed young man. He takes a slow breath, clears his throat, and in a soft voice answers, "It was Mary, my son. Your dear mother's name was Mary."

MELODY

This story, I'm thinking, is like the gray spider dangling an arm's length from where I sit. I admire the resourcefulness of spiders. They're so self-sufficient – a good quality in this day and age. One single thread supports the spider and its eight-legged dance, so the material must be strong even though it looks like almost nothing. I wonder – about the spider and the story. Will they land? Will they be blown off-course? Will they survive?

I can't say this is my story. My life has been mundane, centered on routines – not good narrative material. Even so, I've decided to take breaks every now and again during the day and settle here at my little all-purpose table by the window to write things down. I'm not so much creating or composing as daydreaming, then reporting what pops into my head.

When I put it like that, it occurs to me that it's the same way I made up songs when I was a kid. Yes, that's a good place to start. My mother, Vera, told me this bit of personal history plenty of times over the years, and a good thing too, otherwise details would be ridiculously fuzzy, knowing my old brain.

She would have been driving along with me in one of those booster chairs in the backseat. I was four, five, maybe going on six, heading to pre-school or kindergarten if it was a weekday during the school year, or to some day camp or Grandma Vi's place over weekends or vacations.

Vera was always going to work. Always, always. It felt like there was a big dark hole in my chest where a lot of mommy stuff was supposed to be. People insisted I smile. Sure. Easier said than done. I didn't even call her Mom or Mommy. It was Vera.

Anyway, from my perch in the backseat, I'd study what I could see of her – one shoulder, side of neck and head, hands on the steering wheel, a slice of cheekbone and eyes in the rearview mirror. Tight, all tight. Kinda scary. Looking at her too long gave me a stomach ache. Kids always remember what gave them stomach aches.

So I squirmed and swiveled as much as I could against the straps that held me, and I made myself look out the side window. With all my might, I concentrated on shapes zooming by, and colors streaming, and the pulsing of light and shadow, until all of a sudden my brain switched off. Or maybe it opened up, I don't know. But in that empty zone – Vera figured it lasted ten or fifteen minutes – a complete song would come to me. I'm pretty sure that the ideas for the lyrics were prompted by things I'd seen out the window or heard from the car radio or one of Vera's business calls on her cell phone. But she swore I definitely wasn't mimicking or repeating. In fact, more often it seemed to her that my songs were arguing back, insisting on another point of view.

When Vera combed through her memories, she could patch together the words of some of my simplest ditties – one about the earth breathing, one about animals needing more space, one about worms in the compost, one about quiet being preferable to noise. Forget about the tunes. She was pretty tone-deaf.

But she knew, and I know, there was one song that changed everything. It went:

There's no such thing as a smokestack.
There's no such thing as a tailpipe.
There's no such thing as a cooling tower.
Just wind and sun and water – blowing, shining, flowing.

There's no such thing as pollution.
There's no such thing as garbage.
There's no such thing as a pipeline.
Just wind and sun and water – blowing, shining, flowing.

When I started singing it through a second time, my usually stony-faced and distracted mother, whose typical response to anything I said or sang was "Mmm-hmm," instead pulled over to the shoulder of the road, shut off the engine, turned, and stared at me.

It made me nervous. "What?" I said.

Her expression kept changing, and she had to move her mouth around before any words came out. "Umm. Yeah. Did Grandma Vi teach you that song?"

"Grandma Vi? Whaddya mean?"

"Nothing. Never mind," she said. Then she faced front and slumped. Her whole body went soft, and she sighed and sighed and sighed.

When I started to cry in confusion, she elbowed her door open, climbed in the backseat beside me, unhooked all my safety buckles, and pulled me into her lap – an unheard-of action on her part. What I clearly remember is that she whispered this into my hair – "Melody. Little Melody. You are living up to your name."

Names are significant in this story. Of course, that realization has come with decades of hindsight. I'm sure no one in the generations of my family named a child in a fortune-telling, prophetic sort of way. That would be creepy. Maybe we've all just lived up to our names.

It starts with my great-grandmother's name, Vivian – like from Latin or French for "to live" – Vivere / Vivre. All I know of her story is that she was about eight or nine in the late 1930s when her family was attempting to escape Eastern Europe. She's the only one that made it. Vivere / Vivre, indeed. From what Grandma Vi told me, Vivian never talked much at all, much less reminiscing about her family. Well no wonder, I figure.

Apparently, when I was really little, I met her a few times. But the only occasion I recall was when Grandma Vi and Vera and I went to see her in the nursing home shortly before she died. My mother and grandmother sat at the sides of her bed, each holding one of her hands. I sat across the room, noticing the way the light slanted through the window blinds and lit her up. She was translucent. I could see the sunshine go right through her.

Way back in 1952, when Great-grandmother Vivian was a young married woman, still feeling like a stranger in this country, she named her baby daughter Violet after the precious small flower that had carpeted the ground around her Eastern European home. I feel guilty that I don't even know what country she came from. It just shows how easily history can disappear. But I love it that she transplanted those cherished blossoms here, into her child.

Of course, Grandma Vi took that name and did her own thing with it. She was a hippie in the '60s and '70s and even into the '80s. Everything she wore was tie-dyed purple and scented with essential oil – probably violet, knowing her. I don't think she was into the drug scene, but apparently she loved to demonstrate. That frightened her mother, Vivian, who'd seen the horrors of a repressive regime and had grown up trying to be invisible. Not Grandma Vi. As she put it, she was full of piss and vinegar and had a deep need to be alternative. She marched in various capital cities, wrote letters to editors and government leaders, participated in sit-ins on campuses, and helped organize massive protests against the big polluters around her hometown.

My mother, Vera, had lots of uncomfortable memories of

growing up in a granola and tofu household, being taken along to demonstrations, being dressed in what she called psychedelic colors. She was mortified by the whole thing. She admitted to me that, more than once, she yelled at her mother that she just wanted to live a normal life.

Now, about her name. Grandma Vi was a big fan of Greenpeace, any country that had an official Green Party, and the French language. That's why she named my mother "Vera." "Vera" is like "vert," the French word for green. My grandmother was always saying "Voila" and "C'est la vie" and "Merde," so that's about all the French I know.

But Vera's response to her mother's "Ooh la la" was to take Latin in school, and she told her mother that "vera" was Latin for "the facts." She signed up for sciences and debate club. She insisted on shopping for her own clothes, all in navy, gray, black, and white. Once she started university, she worked and got her own place so she wouldn't have to go home over holidays. In grad school, she studied corporate law. That made Grandma Vi cringe, I bet. She'd spent her life fighting corrupt and irresponsible corporations, and there was her daughter, aiding and abetting.

That's something else that changed the day I sang my smokestack song. It's obvious to me now why Vera thought maybe Grandma Vi had taught it to me. Goodness knows I'd heard my grandmother rant about pipelines and cooling towers and garbage. But the day my mother climbed in the backseat of the car with me, she knew, but I'd not yet heard, that Grandma Vi had been diagnosed with a rare cancer that had a ridiculously high rate of incidence among the current and former residents of her polluted hometown.

My mother was shaken. She'd done work for some of those

companies. She'd helped them fight and win cases against environmentalists. As I sat on her lap that day in the car, she told me Grandma Vi was busy and needed a break on weekends. She didn't let on that her mom was bald and puking.

It was later, when my grandmother had started to feel human again and her hair had partially grown back, that Vera said Grandma Vi had been pretty sick so I'd need to be mellow during visits. At that, I started to sing that old Donovan song – *They call me Mellow Yellow, quite rightly...* I interrupted myself at one point to say, "Oh yeah, Grandma Vi did teach me this song." Vera laughed so hard she got the hiccoughs, because it turns out that when Vera was a girl, she and Grandma Vi danced around their apartment to that record. When she'd calmed back down, she said in a talking-to-herself sort of way, "Those were about the only times we got along."

Grandma Vi's health continued to improve, and I was convinced it was because I continued to sing *Mellow Yellow*. I sang it not only in the backseat, probably driving Vera crazy, but also while sitting on what I called my special rock in the backyard of our place. I was a weird kid, I suppose – not interested in games or sports or music lessons or even in playing with other kids much. But I loved that rock. It got warm in the sun, and from there I felt like I could see the whole world – wildflowers of all colors, trees of all shapes and sizes, hills and creeks and ponds, bugs and birds and garter snakes and clouds. Vera once told me I looked like a little Buddha sitting there. When I asked, "What's that?" she bought one of those fat smiling statues that was almost as big as I was and set it up on another rock near mine. I sang. It smiled. We had a nice symbiotic relationship.

After the smokestack song incident, Vera came outside more often rather than just checking on me through the kitchen window. Together, we set up bird feeders and planted big pots of bright flowers to keep the bees happy. Sometimes we had picnics. I feel as though I'm gushing here, but that's what happens when dark holes in little girl chests start to fill and brighten.

Vera's career change had a lot to do with this improvement. She was still working almost as many hours, but she'd switched over to handling cases for environmental organizations. She wasn't tight any more. She was pumped – maybe still a little intense as a mother, but at least she no longer gave me stomach aches.

One day when she dropped me at Grandma Vi's on her way to work, she took her mother's hand – another unheard-of action – and said she'd rethought the meaning of her name. Rather than "the facts" it was more like "the truth."

Grandma Vi said, "Oh, Vera Honey," and got teary.

So I said, "What? What?" until they both hugged me, which made me forget my question.

Vera and my dad, Jack, named me Melody because neither of them could carry a tune, although they loved music. I turned out to be the singing-est kid ever. But except when I was participating in a school choir, I was geeky and socially awkward, so of course when it came time to name my own child, I named her Grace.

By now, the metaphor of the spider's web might be making some sense. This is the story of a thin line of only-children – all girls. It's strange, I know. Vivian, I'm guessing, only had one child, because that's all she knew she could save if her world fell apart again. Violet only had one, because she never did get married and couldn't afford more as a single hippie mom. Vera and Jack had just me, because they were both so busy being type-A.

I was born in 2000, which brings me to the third thing that changed around the time I sang my smokestack song. Again, hindsight makes things clearer. In her new job, Vera was sure that her work to protect the environment was making a difference. Governments and some corporations were taking positive action. Lots of people were trying to reduce their carbon footprint. But climate scientists later calculated that we had, in fact, already passed the tipping point – that from the time I sang my little song, we were headed for the abyss.

Before getting pregnant with Grace, who was born in 2023, I seriously questioned the appropriateness of my having children at all. It was abundantly clear to me that there were too many humans on Earth. Crowding was bringing out the meanness in people. But her dad, Raymond, a self-described inter-tribal Dene man, spoke reverently of seven generations.

"Why seven?" I asked. "I'm having trouble thinking past two or three."

"Seven is sacred."

"But why?"

He paused to consider. "I'd say it's about twice as far ahead as any of us can imagine. It makes us stretch into the future."

I liked that idea and thought I should not be the one to cut the thread of continuity. Now, people like me who sew know there are different qualities of thread. Some will break at the slightest tug. Some is tough as sinew. The single strand of my family is surprisingly strong and resilient, and I always say it's because we're a genetic United Nations. Vivian's husband was a Portuguese immigrant who'd also escaped a nasty political situation. Grandma Vi's lover who fathered Vera was African-American. My father Jack's parents were Vietnamese boat people. Like I said, my husband Raymond was aboriginal, and he used to say I looked more Indian than he did. My daughter Grace's partner is Finnish. The two of them, like many other couples of their generation, had difficulty getting pregnant, because wicked toxins in the environment and traumatic stress led to high rates of infertility and miscarriage. But I'm getting ahead of myself here.

I met Raymond at university, and he was my second special rock. I wanted to be in his warm presence. The day we met, he asked about my name. I told him how I had made up songs in the car and how I'd sung while sitting on my backyard rock. But then I explained that, at some point during my teenage years, I'd lost the ability to come up with lyrics. Life had gotten too precarious. Kids I knew from school were committing suicide or ODing or joining hate groups or doing ugly stuff on-line. It felt like I, and everything else, was sliding out of control down an icy mountainside or a loose scree slope. I would open my mouth, and my lungs forced air past my vocal chords. Sometimes I screamed. Sometimes I roared. The few tunes I choked out were like dirges. There were no words available to me.

Raymond told me about power songs and took me to native gatherings and sacred ceremonies. I learned to sing vowels, the parts of words that carry the breath, the spirit. Those songs circulated through me like blood, re-oxygenating my brain. The drumming steadied my feet on the ground and kept me from falling.

We lived together, and I still live, in a small sod-roofed cabin at the corner of my family's property. Our big acreage abutted the reserve of Raymond's people. These days, I wouldn't be able to say where the old borders were. They've been erased and eroded over time – and not just property lines but boundaries between nations and boundaries between land and sea. Every time the climate convulsed, or harvests failed, or fires raged, or violence broke out, people ran for their lives. They ran, and there was nothing that could stop them, especially not invisible lines.

We still had access to news then – radio mostly. But it was hard to listen. The whole world was crazy. More than crazy. That's when Raymond and I established our routines. That's how we coped and how we stayed sane.

Raymond had grown up learning traditional ways, so he hunted in the fall and trapped and cut firewood during the winter. The gardens and fruit trees and vineyard had seasonal tasks for us, and the goats and chickens, and of course, our young daughter Grace, needed tending daily. When gasoline became unavailable and battery charging stations blacked out, Vera and Jack gave up their condo and their jobs in the city and moved back home and fell into routines, too. Raymond and Jack scrounged all of the alternative power technology and tools they could lay their hands on and fixed us up with solar, wind and micro-hydro stations and a deep well. My parents turned their workaholic tendencies to schooling their granddaughter, beekeeping, seed-saving and, best of all, developing a roof-top garden on the big house I grew up in. That meant more food and better indoor temperature control as well as camouflage from air surveillance. I don't like being paranoid, but there it is. Like my great-grandmother, we were trying to be invisible.

We knew that fear could do us in. Winston Churchill had warned about that way back in Vivian's time. It wasn't easy to be calm and rational, especially when we heard explosions near and far, felt the ground shake, smelled acrid smoke, saw flashes and fireballs in the sky, got battered by vicious storms, and knew ourselves to be more and more isolated when radio broadcasts ended, businesses shut down, government and police services no longer functioned, and neighbors – poof – just disappeared. We desperately needed other routines besides just those connected to providing food, clothing and shelter.

So every single morning, Raymond and I went outside to greet the day with a prayer that looked ahead seven generations, and every evening we went out again to give thanks. All over the property, when rocks were cleared from garden plots and fields, we formed spirals and labyrinths, and when solid stumps remained after tree-felling, we turned them into medicine wheels and altars. When we gathered wild edibles and medicines, we sang power songs and left offerings. We smudged ourselves, our home, and my special rock and the Buddha statue. We talked to, and welcomed insects, birds, and animals, and we noticed that some migratory species were staying put, right on our place, year-round. Most importantly, on solstices and equinoxes, we walked the entire perimeter of the land we worked and cared for, imagining the life within protected by an obscuring and impermeable energetic field.

And just in case that wasn't enough, we beefed up physical security by transplanting thorny wild roses and stinging nettle and devil's club and tangles of alder trees around the entire place. That was a hellacious job. But then we watched in wonder as the plants sprang to our defense. They grew taller, thicker, pricklier, and far more impenetrable than we'd ever seen anywhere else. Raymond kept one narrow, and hard to detect, passageway open during those decades when we still ventured out for trading or fishing or scavenging or gathering. Then one day, Raymond went out to set nets in the river and never came back. I waited at that gap in the thicket until I collapsed. Vera and Jack, almost seventy by then, somehow managed to carry me back to the house. The passageway is probably all overgrown now. I don't know. When

I walk by that spot four times a year during my perimeter walk, I have to do it with my eyes closed.

Grace, who also grew into her name in her own way, was on tour with her newest dance-theater production when Raymond disappeared, and she asked if she should come home to help me. I told her absolutely not. I use the words "she asked" and "I told" so blithely, but communications had become almost impossible. It was satellite technology or nothing, and my hook-up was sketchy. She and her husband Jan had a fairly reliable link since they traveled the world by air-bot. They flew under cover of darkness from safe-zone to safe-zone, to share their art – part therapy, part message, part catalyst. When I first saw my adult daughter perform via video link, I was reminded of the wind, sun and water of my childhood song – blowing, shining, flowing. It did cross my mind that their work, like Vera's in environmental law, might have come too late. Then I said to myself, "Screw that." In both cases, it was the right thing to do, and that's all there is to it.

But back to the call from Grace. I'll never forget it – not just because we were able to actually hear each other, and not just because of her generous offer to come home, but because of her announcement. A month or two earlier, she and Jan had been presenting their show and workshops in Nepal, or in what had once been called Nepal. One evening they went up to sit on their host family's flat rooftop. Whether because of the high elevation or a sudden shift in air currents, the heavens, which had for over a decade been obscured by unbroken gray-brown murkiness, cleared enough for them to see a band of silky black space, studded with silver stars. They conceived their long-wished-for child that night. My daughter told me, with a smile in her voice, that they would name the baby Sky.

And what did my grand-daughter do with that name? After years of being schooled by her parents in the course of their travels, she marched up to a recruiter visiting safe-zones, applied, and was accepted at one of the few secure educational facilities in the world – the Global Aeronautics and Space Campus.

That Sky! She's a bright spark. Having access to the best technology and well-equipped space lab networks, she set up reliable computer links with Grace and Jan, wherever they might find themselves, and with me here. Always here. That saved me. I'd been all alone for a few years by then – since my parents had died. The only home I'd ever known had become a solitary confinement cell – until she reached out to me.

She'd signal that she was about to show up on my screen with a chorus of *Mellow Yellow*. That song sure has staying power in our family. Her smiling face would pop up, and she'd say, "How ya doin', Grandma Melo?" Like I used to call Violet Grandma Vi. It gave me such a kick.

I got to share in all her news as she graduated with highest honors, served on missions at several of the space stations, and worked for a while at colonies on the moon and Mars troubleshooting technological stuff. It's really something having a family of scientists, artists, environmental activists, and farmers. That's one healthy mix, I'd say.

Yes, "scientists" is plural. Sky and Ravi, from India or what was once called India, met during their first year on the campus, and that was it. Just like it was for me and Raymond. They didn't plan on having children – the idea was considered kind of an occupational hazard – but sometimes fate is in the stars, literally. They were receiving training updates at one of the launch sites when they got confirmation of Sky's pregnancy. They had to do some fast thinking. Bone density is negatively affected by changes in gravity, hard enough on adult bodies, potentially disastrous for children. So they worked out a brilliant combination of parental leaves, alternating missions, and teaching and consulting via satellite from home.

And guess where home is? Here with me. Well, not just me. Grace and Jan have retired here and have fixed up my parents' old house, half for themselves and half for their daughter's family. I flipped the night they, unannounced, landed the air-bot in the lower field. I was sitting on my special rock, getting chilled, tired to the bone, sure I couldn't manage by myself much longer. The house was getting run-down, the gardens overgrown, and I wasn't eating or sleeping well. I'd say that the old thread I was hanging from was just about to snap.

But there's that strong family line for you. Some days I wake up and say out loud, "Oh, yeah, I have help now." That help includes Irene, who just turned five. Sky and Ravi named her that because it means "peace" in Greek. I won't be around to see what she does with her name, but that's okay. I feel more peaceful right now than I have since Vera and I had picnics in the back yard.

And speaking of peace, all of us are noticing how much quieter everything seems lately – hardly any more explosions or flashes in the sky. The air doesn't smell so bad. And I hope it's not just a trick of my weakening eyesight, but I'd say the murky sky is clearing. Maybe there are no more tailpipes, smokestacks, or cooling towers out there. Maybe my song has come true. Wouldn't that be something?

When she's on duty in one of the space stations, my granddaughter reports that she's making more frequent contact with people in safe-zones as satellite systems are getting patched back together after that last big solar storm. And with the high-powered scopes, she's able to zoom in on Earth's surface through gaps in the pollution layer and search for evidence of other tiny oases like ours. They'd show up as little freckles of green against the brown skin of the planet, the kind of contrast it's possible to detect from space, she tells us.

I wish Raymond could be here to see this. "Hey, Raymond," I whisper towards the clouds. "Look – seven generations. Right here on the place. Right here in my mind. Talk about sacred." It turns out that Great-grandmother Vivian's ashes are buried underneath my special rock. I never knew, when I was a kid, why the words "Vivere / Vivre" were carved into it. That's my mother's Latin and my grandmother's French paying tribute. Grandma Vi's ashes were scattered in the backyard as my parents and I danced to *Mellow Yellow* and, believe it or not, a field of violets has grown up there around Vivian. Vera and Jack's ashes fertilized the roof-top garden, and it is still as compulsively productive as they were. Then there's me, Grace and Jan, Sky and Ravi, and Irene.

The hazy sun is shining in the window by my little table, and when it hits the spider's strand, now anchored on the window's lower sill, it shimmers with color. The spider apparently moved on when I wasn't looking, and now I have to get going, too. It's time to check on my great-granddaughter, and I know just where to look for her. Irene has adopted my special rock as her own and says she can see the whole world from there. She sings the song we made up together. It's called *Seven Generations on Seven Continents.* When she sits there, Buddha-like, she is translucent. I swear, the light shines right through her.

MELENA'S SON

Martin swung his last two suitcases into the wheelbarrow to take them down to the boat landing then called to his mother who stood, arms crossed, in the doorway. "Don't expect me for dinner!" He laughed and could hear that his voice was too shrill, too sharp.

That was the line he and his dad always tossed off at their weekly departures into town even though all three of them knew that between the twenty minute boat ride to what they called the civilized side of the lake where there were roads and other houses, the forty-five minute drive into town, the hours spent doing laundry and errands, the leisurely coffee times with buddies, all of the loading and unloading, and the return trip, there was no way, even if they set out right after breakfast, that they'd get home before eight p.m.

His mom had her regular replies, too, like, "Come in quietly. I might be asleep," even though she was a night owl, or "I'll make us a nightcap," even though she didn't drink. But this time she said nothing. Martin thought she'd at least be trying to joke, but no, she looked mad as hell. She'd told him a month earlier when she sent off her mail-in ballot, that she'd voted for one of the people running against him.

He waited until the nervous laugh quit quaking his chest then walked to her and kissed her cheek. "I love you, Mom," he said. "Don't worry."

"Sure," she replied.

He trotted away down the slope, trying to release the shoulder tension that was making it hard to control the wheelbarrow around the ruts and potholes in the trail. He caught himself thinking he'd have to get out the shovel to do some leveling in the next couple of weeks before the ground froze then realized that this time he wouldn't be back after a day of errands. Giving attention to ruts and potholes in roads throughout the territory would more likely be one of his jobs as a new member of the legislative assembly. It seemed unreal.

His dad, Jake, had already loaded his other boxes and bags into the motorboat and had the tarp tied down except for the corner where the two suitcases would nestle. He was whistling and grinning as Martin approached the dock.

"Looks like your mom's got a burr up her butt," he said. "She figures her baby boy's gone over to the dark side."

Probably, thought Martin. She was as green and far-left-liberal as they come, and he'd turned out to be the conservative's young poster boy. It was his dad's friends that got him to run, that convinced a lot of people to vote for him. He'd always been a favorite of theirs – hanging on their words and stories at the coffee shops in town or around campfires in the bush. And he liked being with them. They had big voices and big laughs. They always were saying that being a good listener was an essential quality in a politician and assured him he had the right stuff.

Everything loaded into the boat, Martin and Jake put on life jackets, climbed aboard and pushed off. They turned to wave at Martin's mom, still standing at the door, but she didn't wave back.

"Oh Melena, Melena," said Jake, shaking his head. "You are a piece of work." Then he turned to his son. "Did she give you a hard time?"

"No, not a hard time." He pressed his lips together. "It's just a drag that this is the most amazing thing that's ever happened to me and she hates it."

"Never mind," Jake said. "You just run with it. You're going somewhere more interesting than our far side of the lake."

Martin, for all his excitement about his future in politics, had a moment of doubt about his dad's statement. Their side of the lake still seemed like the best place on earth to him. The log house at the top of the knoll looked west over the deep cold lake that, in summer, reflected mountains and late sunsets and people having fun in boats. On their property, six small tourist cabins were tucked into the edge of the forest, each with its own name and animal emblem carved on a sign over the door. As a teenager, he'd made those with care and pride during what his dad had called "shop class". The cabins were full all summer, and a few were available for the winter season, too. Jake was great at sharing the outdoors with people – paddling, bird-watching, photography, hunting, mushing, northern-lights-watching. You name it. Martin had helped him with all of it since he was twelve when his dad became his school teacher, and the business, and people skills, became part of his education.

Melena was a full partner in the operation, but the guests hardly saw her. She kept the cabins in top condition and put veritable feasts out on the buffet table for meals at the lodge or in a big cooler for lunches on the go. She had home-schooled Martin through his elementary years giving him an excellent grounding in the three Rs. She filled his mind with stories and songs and images and curious questions. Martin wondered why that felt like a lifetime ago. These days, his mother spent much of each day in her studio, where she wrote and painted. Her books were for sale on the gift rack by the registration desk as well as at outlets in town, the territory's small capital city.

Jake put his hand on Martin's shoulder as they neared the public boat ramp on the shore opposite their home. He pulled at his son's jacket collar, inspecting its frayed edge. "I'm going to have to buy you a new suit so you don't go into the legislature looking like a scruffy country kid."

The next week was totally nuts. Martin had no idea that one human could be expected to attend so many meetings. But with all of the planning and team-building came an increased comfort level with his fellow conservative caucus members. Their big voices and big laughs reassured him.

Meanwhile, he'd had to buy more clothes, and a heap of wrinkled, smelly, but unfrayed shirts was piling up on the floor of his rental condo. The new job was making him sweat more than usual. "It's pretty intense," he told his dad when they went out for coffee at one of their quieter haunts. Jake clued him in that the laundromat they'd frequented for years was also a cleaners where he could just drop off his dirty clothes and pick them up later, good as new. Thank God, thought Martin, for guys with more life experience who could give him advice. He felt so naïve sometimes.

So Martin was shocked when the new premier chose him as minister of the environment based on his work experience and his family's good reputation as wilderness tourism operators. As minister, he'd have to stand up and talk and sound like he was brimming with confidence. And he had thought he could just get away with being a good listener? Sheesh.

For days, he practiced speaking, pacing the length of his condo, as if forming words was something he'd never done before. He kept his voice low-pitched and calm. He added gestures for emphasis. He made sure he stood up straight. He started many of his sentences with the words, "Let me be perfectly clear."

First thing in the morning on the day the fall sitting was to open, he got himself the most expensive haircut he'd ever had and put on the suit Jake had bought him. He stood in front of the mirror and couldn't believe the jacket pulled a bit across the belly. Shit. Since the whole election process started, he hadn't been getting enough exercise, and he certainly hadn't been eating as healthily as he would at home. He tightened his abs, lifted his chest, and pulled in his chin. Shit again. An extra chin pouched out below his jaw. He turned to check out the profile view and uttered the third shit in a row. His neatly trimmed temples showed the first sprinkling of gray.

He grabbed his briefcase and coffee mug and headed out the door fifteen minutes earlier than he'd planned to. He left his car in the garage and walked the ten blocks to the government building. He thought about the older men around town who'd encouraged him to run for office or who'd been helping him learn the ropes of his new job. Which of them could he ask about hair dye and gym memberships?

He felt better the minute he walked into his caucus area. There was his team. Hands clapped him on the back. That helped. The nervous energy in his belly transformed into a feeling of strength and purpose in his neck, back and shoulders. Everything was going to be okay. He was pumped. He felt grown up.

As he bowed toward the speaker's chair and strode to his seat in the front row, aware of the rolling cameras, he worked hard to keep up the power stance. It wasn't as easy before the eyes of the opposition, and visitors in the gallery, as it had been behind the scenes. He told himself he could manage it for the four hours of the session.

Martin sat in the big cushy chair at his designated place and arranged a few papers and folders. He noticed that others were leaning back comfortably and scanning the gallery for familiar faces. One member of his team actually crossed the floor to greet and shake hands with members of the minority parties. He wished he had the chutzpah to do that.

He sat ramrod straight and opened a folder without seeing what it was. Instead he saw his mother, Melena, across the dinner table, looking at him with disbelief, grilling him. Why would a young man, raised in nature, skilled in all things outdoorsy, quiet and artistic and sensitive, even consider a career in politics? Why would he want a job where his public and private lives would be constantly scrutinized? How would he reconcile the values he'd been taught at home with the business-above-all values of his chosen party? How would he feel having to promote dirty resource extraction projects after having grown up in pristine wilderness? He didn't know the answers. Running for office, for him, was about being around people he liked, not so much about issues. So he'd kept saying, "It'll work. It'll be fine," until she'd thrown up her hands and said, "Martin Edward Lewis, it drives me crazy when you answer like a programmed automaton instead of a thinking human being."

Now here he sat in a potentially worse hot seat, and among the papers in front of him were prepared statements he'd been told to read and repeat if necessary during question period. He hoped Melena wasn't listening to the proceedings on the radio at home while she painted.

He looked up to see that all the members opposite and the speaker had taken their places. And looking right back at him was another Melena. Melena Richards. He'd had a good laugh about her having the same name, as well as the same political leanings, as his mother when he saw her campaign posters and had laughed even harder when she'd handily won a seat in the official opposition. But now laughing was the farthest thing from his mind. Her posters hadn't done her justice. She was gorgeous. He squirmed. She smiled. Could she be laughing at him?

A few weeks into the sitting, he'd gotten used to the prescribed way of speaking and the usual poking and jabbing across the floor. He felt the same as when he'd finally learned to swim after years of thrashing and splashing. In the legislative assembly, as in the pool, he just had to remind himself to breathe smoothly and regularly. But he still couldn't bring himself to lounge back in his chair.

His mother's question about how he'd feel when faced with the issue of resource extraction was haunting him. It was so weird to be environment minister and not be working collaboratively with environmental groups. Oh, he met with them and made the soothing statements that had been scripted for him, but he knew, and knew that they knew, that the decisions were being made by the premier and the minister of energy, mines and resources. They'd been talking big money with oil and gas lobbyists and had told Martin, with good-natured slaps on the back, to come up with as many ways as possible to babble about open consultation and safety standards and funding for clean-up without promising anything.

When he had to stand and answer questions in the legislature, he couldn't help noticing that Melena Richards, seated across from him, had lost her smile and was looking at him with his mother's air of disbelief. He started taking antacid after sessions and a sleeping aid at bedtime.

The parks and wilderness association folks called a press conference to express their frustration in dealing with him, minister of the environment, and his whole team. They'd started a petition to ban fracking in the territory, and word on the street was that it was getting lots of signatures. Martin had a spooky thought that if he were still living on the other side of the lake, he might sign it. He scoffed, told himself he was misremembering his younger self. But it made him nervous to learn that Ms. Richards would be presenting the petition to the assembly and would introduce a bill to enforce the ban – a ban that ran counter to his party's efforts.

That day, Martin couldn't eat his lunch. He had to change shirts fifteen minutes before the house opened. During the preliminaries, he stood to read a tribute to a team of fisheries scientists who had just visited the territory and praised the clean waterways. He heard his own voice as a tired drone. He plopped into his chair and unbuttoned his jacket which seemed tighter than ever across his belly. He wished he could loosen his tie, too. Breathe, he told himself. He shuffled papers from one side of his desk to the other. His eyes felt gritty, and he wondered how he could lay his hands on some drops in a hurry.

When Melena Richards started her speech, he was startled by the power in her voice. It flowed like a wide fast river, and Martin saw himself and his cohorts as menacing rocks that her words, like water, could just flow over and around, gradually wearing them away. She had obviously done her homework. She quoted more facts and figures and supporting research than he had ever heard from a politician before. When she added that the idea of fracking made her feel physically ill, Martin found himself nodding in understanding. Then he heard the snickers and whispers around him and turned to see his fellow conservatives rolling their eyes and chuckling. He mirrored their grins, and his face felt like a clown mask. He rubbed his cheeks.

He rubbed his temples. He felt a headache coming on.

Martin hated how the minister of energy, mines and resources spoke to Melena Richards and other members of the opposition. He twisted things to make it sound as though they were intent on ruining the economy or creating a climate of fear or pushing outsiders' environmental agendas. Martin knew this was just posturing. When the EMR minister and the premier put their heads together and whispered behind their hands, he was pretty sure they were just pretending to have something top secret to say to each other. Having listened to their banter behind the scenes, he guessed they were talking about hockey.

Martin asked the young page to refill his water glass and bring him some aspirin. Then suddenly he realized the session was wrapping up, and there wouldn't be time for a vote. Good, he thought. He didn't want to stand up any more, listen any more, speak any more. He just wanted to take off his suit and tie, lie down in a dark room, and empty all the thoughts from his pounding head. He wished he could magic himself to the far side of the lake.

He imagined himself walking up the trail toward one golden light shining from the kitchen window of the log house on the knoll. Inside that vision, he opens the door to the reception area and smells the fruits and spices of muffins for tomorrow's breakfast.

"How about a nightcap?" his mother calls from around the corner, and they both chuckle. She comes into view and kisses his cheek.

He looks at her steaming cup. "Wild chamomile?" he asks. "Perfect." They sit at the counter and the kitchen is very quiet, very warm. His mother's face is glowing and open and full of stories like the moon.

Back in the legislature, Martin's eyes jerked open, and he shuffled papers one last time even though he was the only one besides the security guard left in the room. He felt like an old man as he rose from his cushy seat. He knew that if he did much of a bow toward the speaker's chair, he might not be able to straighten back up again.

He made his way down the hall to his office, tossed papers on his desk, ignored the blinking message light on his phone, and grabbed his coat but didn't put it on. He shouldered open the building's side door and walked around the back toward the riverside park. The cold air settled him after the dead air of the halls of government. He didn't put his coat on until he started to shiver.

"Martin, how are you?" said a voice, the voice he'd listened to all afternoon, even when, for the sake of appearances, he pretended not to. He looked up to see Melena Richards walking his way.

"What are you doing?" he hissed and squinted into every shadow.

"Don't worry," she said, coming closer. He backed away from her beauty. "I scoped out the scene. What a weird business we're in."

"I shouldn't be talking to you!" Martin had to wonder for a moment if this was one of the scripted lines he'd been directed to say.

"That's what I mean. Weird, right? But really, how are you? You didn't look so good in today's session."

Martin crossed his arms and studied her face. "Melena is my mother's name."

"Oh, I know! I took art classes from her three years in a row when I was a kid. I just loved her!"

"You did?" He tilted his head side to side, imagining her as a paint-smeared lanky-limbed youngster. He turned to walk along the river toward the playground area. "Anyway, thanks for asking. I'm fine now. Everything's fine."

She fell in beside him. "Except?"

"Except what?" Martin stopped in his tracks and faced her. The street lights had come on and were casting double and triple shadows at their feet.

"That's what I'm wondering."

Martin threw his hands in the air, and six shadow arms jumped around him. "What are we doing here? Talking politics? You trying to get something out of me?"

"No. Not that."

"Well, what then?" He paced three steps back and forth in front of her. "You want me to tell you my job is giving me headaches, not to mention indigestion and insomnia?"

"Hmmm, some back pain, too?"

Martin froze and felt all the bluster, all the pumped up shoulder and neck and back energy get sucked right out of him. "You can tell?" It wasn't good to be so readable, not in this line of work. His mother had always known what he was feeling too. He was back in the deep-end of the pool, floundering.

"I watch you," Melena said matter-of-factly. "Probably no one else notices." She led the way this time, and he felt young and bumbling, like a clumsy pup, as he followed. They walked among trees and porta-potties and climbing structures.

"You watch me?"

"Yeah, sometimes." Her hand came up to cover a smile, and Martin stiffened, wondering if he had been wrong to relax in her presence, if she was laughing at him again.

But she sounded serious when she said, "From what I've

seen, I'm guessing you'd like to be a real minister of the environment."

Martin shook his head slowly. "I am minister of the environment." There was that dull robotic voice again.

Melena shook her head right back at him, her chin jutting forward. "You hate it when the EMR minister jumps up and answers for you. You hate having to stifle your natural reactions. You nodded today when I said the idea of fracking made me feel sick. I guess what I meant a moment ago was, you'd like to be minister FOR the environment." He saw her expression change as she paused. She looked sad. "But you can't." Then it changed again. Her eyebrows shot up.

"What? What are you talking about?" Martin demanded.

"You can't... unless you cross the floor."

He gaped and choked on his next inhalation. "Cross the floor. Be an independent." He coughed until his neck was red. "Let down my dad's friends? Piss off everyone who voted for me?"

"Maybe, maybe not." Melena shrugged. "Are you representing your constituents when you read prepared statements?"

The wind went out of Martin as though she'd punched him in the gut. He stumbled around a fountain and a bouncy toy and sat heavily on a swing. "Sorry," he heard from somewhere behind him. "That was harsh."

Martin walked his feet three steps backward, picked them up, and swung till the momentum died. He walked backward again, swung again. He felt Melena nearby, watching. "I haven't been on a swing since I was a kid. We have one at the lake," he said. He remembered his mom singing, "Would you like to swing on a star? Carry moonbeams home in a jar. And be better off than you are…"

He arced back and forth, and the rhythm turned into the murmur of two Melenas' voices saying, "Across the lake, across the floor, across the lake, across the floor."

Suddenly the chains jerked, and he felt the swing being drawn back, then a heave against his lower back. He twisted and twitched. "What the heck? Are you pushing me?"

Melena gave the swing a second, even bigger, shove. "You need a push, don't you?" Then she was gone, headed toward the bus stop.

Martin slammed his feet down on the ground, watched her retreating back and muttered, "What the heck was that all about?" then louder, "What the heck?" At that, she turned and waved. Once she was out of sight, he faced front, stepped backward, and let go again. But this time he leaned far back and pumped his legs for all he was worth.

MELINDA

A father, Roberto, used his finger to draw two trees in the dirt just outside the door of the dwelling. He did this to instruct his daughter, Melinda, which he pronounced "May-leen-da." It means "my pretty one" in his mother tongue. He named her the first time he laid eyes on her, moments after her birth fifteen years before.

The branches of one of the trees represented the generations of his family, and the branches of the other showed Melinda's mother's family. On each limb were the initials of relations' names. The topmost branches of the two trees reached toward each other and met in a heart shape, which pleased the girl. Within that heart were the letters M and R for Melinda and her father as well as S and C for the girl's mother and older brother. Roberto sometimes tested his daughter to see if she remembered all of the names on the trees. She consistently made him proud.

The two of them would then gather leaves from nearby trees and bushes. Reverently, they laid a leaf on top of the initials of each family member dead or lost because of war. This included the S and C within the heart. Melinda and her father stood side by side to study the drawings in the dirt. "So much death makes the trees look alive," the girl said.

Another picture was in Roberto's right hand. He held it out, palm up, to show her the map. The thumb was pressed against the side of his hand and pointer finger, and the pointer stretched long and straight and separate from the other three, which

Roberto held snugly together. The mound at the base of his thumb was the high country where they lived. The creases of his palm were the rivers that flowed to the sea between his middle and pointer fingers. That long bay, those rivers, and the flat plain at the center of his hand were the deadly highways of invaders and rogue mercenaries. War was a constant in the lowlands, he often told her.

She pointed to the deep valley between his thumb and palm. "And here is where war orphans go."

"How do you know this?" he asked sharply.

She blinked and shook her head then whispered, "All children say so." He wrapped his arms around her, and his breath came in uneven gasps above her head.

But her thoughts were still on the map, so she twisted sideways and lifted his hand into view again. "Where did you come from, Father, before you met Mother?"

He took a step backward, walked his left fingers up his right arm, over his shoulder and as far down his back as he could reach. This made her laugh until she saw the lines of sorrow on his face. "Your mother found me after the crossing. She is the only reason I am alive."

He was so still then that Melinda felt frightened and alone. She shook his sleeve, and he shook himself. "War is a predator, like a wolf," he said, hardly moving his lips. "If you run away, it will chase you." He closed his eyes tight, and Melinda could see his eyeballs darting side to side under the lids, could see his throat jerk as he swallowed hard.

Even though their family had lived simply and quietly, as far from others as they could, Melinda's mother had been snatched away by soldiers on horseback one day. It happened so quickly it did not seem real. For weeks, the girl kept expecting her mother to reappear just as suddenly. A few months later, her brother had been forced to march off with a heavily armed band. As far as anyone in the highlands knew, no one who had been taken ever returned.

The two who were left behind, broken-hearted, chose not to run away. They took practical measures to control their fear so the wolf of war would not be able to sniff them out.

Roberto and Melinda took down all of the fences that had defined their homestead and let the wilderness reclaim their garden. They butchered their livestock and dried all of the meat. They became hunters and gatherers of food like their long-ago ancestors had been. "War erases civilization," Roberto lamented time and again. They abandoned and demolished the house from which the lovely S and the brave C had been abducted and reused the biggest and most solid beams to support the heavy sod roof of a much smaller shelter that leaned, and disappeared, into the base of a cliff. Minimally chiseled stones were fitted together to build a false wall at the rear of their spring house, creating a secret space in which to store provisions.

Most important of all, in their efforts to combat fear, they agreed on three nearby hiding places. A dense thicket, a narrow and craggy ravine, and a hollow tree were each furnished with an armful of straw and a skin bag of water. From within, it would be possible to hear the arrivals and departures of strangers, or their agreed-upon low-whistled signal to each other.

Melinda was almost sixteen on the morning that, soon after Roberto had gone off hunting, she heard approaching horses and harsh speech. She ran to the nearest hiding place, squeezed herself into the hollow of the tree, and prayed that the sounds would move on by. But they halted. Horses stamped. Voices shouted triumphantly, cursed and cheered. There was scuffling, banging, thumping, and she jumped at each noise. Then came a crackle and a whoosh. She smelled smoke, and her tears tasted gray. She slid down to a crouch on the straw and put her forehead on her knees.

It's so easy to hear danger but so difficult to hear safety. She tried to convince herself that her home would not burn, being topped with sod and built against the cliff. Whatever the case might be, she couldn't face it alone, so she remained in the hiding place, straining her senses. When she heard her father's whistled signal a few hours later, she rejoiced and tried to uncurl, to uncramp her limbs as quickly as she could. Then her name, called with desperation, squeezed her by the throat, and she coughed and coughed as she stumbled out of the opening. Then other sounds – his running feet, a sharp crack crack, a ground-shaking thud, and the boom of her world collapsing.

She ran toward the awful sight of smoking fallen roof beams and her father's lower arm jutting out from beneath. Then, it may have been the wild beating of her heart that sounded like returning horses, and it may have been her own groans of despair that sounded like foreign harsh voices. Whichever it was propelled her onward, past the ruins of the house, on to the thicket just beyond the opposite edge of the clearing, and she crawled in so quickly that thorns pierced her skin.

Scratched and bleeding, filthy and wide-eyed, she lay on the straw. Her mind filled with images of deformed trees with initials on every branch. She saw herself putting a leaf on top of the letter R, and started to tremble uncontrollably.

It was getting dark, and random sounds continued to confuse her. Her shaking got more severe, and she couldn't tell if it was from cold, shock, fear, or grief. She pinched all of the leaves from the inner branches of the thicket, breathed on the backs to moisten them, stuck them on herself, and fell into oblivion.

Hours later, she startled awake to dim light and an empty silence. Then, a vision of yesterday's horror jerked her up to sitting, and she clenched her arms around her knees and rocked back and forth. The motion brought memories of Roberto standing and swaying sadly with her after her mother disappeared. He had done so again when her brother was taken. She pretended, now, that it was he initiating the rocking, that he was, as always, comforting her. Everything Father provided I still have, she thought. She repeated it over and over, to convince herself.

She acknowledged another way he had provided for her when pangs of hunger forced her from the cover of the thicket. Thanks to his skill as a hunter, there was food in the hidden space behind the spring house.

She brushed the leaves from her skin. "I guess I am still alive," she said, resigned. But she did not register that the cuts and scratches that had been covered by leaves had healed overnight.

Melinda approached the wreck of her home feeling as though she might throw up. Would the sight of her father's hand, futilely beseeching heaven or pointing her toward the deep valley of war orphans, send her back to the thicket to hide from the truth?

But she couldn't see his hand, although from the angle of the fallen beam, she knew right where it should appear. Had something else fallen and hidden it? Had soldiers returned and desecrated the body? Or animals? There was a stirring, and she raced toward it, ready to attack whoever or whatever would dare.

Lying on the ground, facing the beam under which Roberto's body lay, was a boy, a young man. He had grasped her father's lifeless hand and laid it upon his own head, as if asking for a blessing or requesting forgiveness. The stiffness of death had molded the man's fingers to the boy's skull. Amazed, Melinda noticed that Roberto's thumb and pointer finger were pressed to each other as were the other three fingers. She felt as though she were being shown a new map.

The boy was in rough shape. His hands were badly cut, blood had soaked through his shirt, and the side of his face was grazed. She was reminded of her own injuries from the night before and, only then, inspecting her arms and legs, realized the thicket's powerful medicinal properties. She hurried to the bush and gathered all the leaves her hands could hold and returned to sit on the ground close to the young man's back.

She laid the greens in her lap, took a steadying breath, and gently covered her father's hand with one of her own. She could feel the boy's curls between her fingers. She placed her other hand on the dirt beside her, where Roberto had often drawn the family trees. She asked all of her ancestors for their help. Then, like nutrients moving upward in a living tree, she felt a flow that started in the earth, coursed warmly through her body, and into her opposite hand. At that, the boy's eyes popped open, and his body stiffened.

"Be still," Melinda said softly. One by one, she breathed on the healing herbs and applied them to his wounds. Only his eyes moved. When she was almost done, she asked, as if she already knew the answer, "Your name starts with C, doesn't it?"

"They call me... called me Chacho."

She considered this. "So now you are my brother."

He nodded, and his head was rubbed by Roberto's hand. Chacho squirmed an inch away from it. "I'm sorry. Forgive me," he said.

Melinda laid the last leaf on the side of his face then put her own hand on his head. She touched her other hand to the dirt and once again said, "Be still." Through her once more came the stream of energy and his eyes widened even further than before. They darted side to side and he swallowed hard over and over as he coughed out pieces of story – being a young boy at the place of war orphans, being handed over to one of the invading armies, being a slave in charge of fire and water and yet kept cold and thirsty. Then yesterday being ordered to light the torch, the torch that one of the men threw into Melinda's home. But Chacho didn't see that part of the story for he had already dashed toward the narrow ravine he'd glimpsed at the base of a craggy outcropping, thrown himself into it, felt the skin scraped from the side of his face, felt his limbs bruised and bloodied. He couldn't believe his good fortune when he found a nest of straw and a skin of water under an overhang. He drank every drop then lay still until he heard the soldiers, after much cursing and crashing, depart. He must have passed out then, because he didn't hear the low whistle, the crack crack thud, her running feet or the circling back of horses, but he could guess all of this, because in the company of those men, he'd seen so much.

When he'd regained consciousness in the dark, his thirst was greater than his pain, and he had crawled out of the ravine and to the spring house. He drank and drank, and it was the taste of freedom. Then the sight of Roberto's hand clenched his throat with sorrow but gave him the gift of one memory from before he was orphaned – the memory of a hand on his head, a touch of love. And so he had placed himself where she had found him. After that, Chacho could speak no more, and the two of them cried together.

When the late morning sun's rays emerged from behind the

hill and warmed their backs, Melinda sat up straight and said, "Come, we must pack up."

The boy raised himself gingerly and touched his face, releasing a shower of greenery. The pain, the roughness, the raw flesh were gone. "Umm, Sister?"

"Melinda," she said, pronouncing it as her father always had. She drew a heart in the dirt below her father's hand, put an R in the middle and covered it with a handful of leaves.

"My pretty one," Chacho said. At her shocked expression, he covered his face in embarrassment. "There is one more detail of the story I should have mentioned. The army that held me all these years was from your father's country. I played dumb all the time around them, but I know their language."

"Well, all right then. But that's no way to talk to a sister." And they found themselves grinning shyly at each other.

She opened up the hidden access to the back of the spring house, took out two large skin packs, and started handing out everything she thought they could carry. "We are not running away from war," Melinda announced as they crammed items into the packs, but she did not elaborate. She showed him the map in her right hand. Chacho knew all the rivers and plains and valleys of war, but he had no knowledge of the high ridge along the thumb, and that was where she was proposing they go. Roberto had not told his daughter anything about that area beyond what could be seen from the map itself – the steep plunging valley between the thumb and palm on one side and the vertical cliffs above the sea on the other. "Difficult to access and difficult to escape in case of danger." – Roberto's words that she now repeated.

"Yes," Chacho said flatly. "And then?"

Melinda shrugged, shaking her head. With the sinking

realization that she truly had no plan, she started to repeat the gesture. But then she froze with her shoulders high and turned her head slowly to the right as if curious. She walked her left fingers up her opposite arm and tapped herself on the shoulder. "My father stood here once."

"I don't think… " But he stopped at her frown. "It's… it's said to be impossible. The steepness, the dangers, the storms, the fog like blindness. I've heard it spoken of. Everyone says that the only way from your father's country to this one is by boat along the coastline."

Her gaze was far away, and she spoke as if from a dream. "He stood here on the mountaintop and, for an hour, the sky, the fog, the clouds over the lands and oceans cleared. He said it could only have been a gift from the gods. He saw the world as they do. And he saw something that maybe no one else has ever seen." She held out the map of her right hand again but this time crossed her left wrist underneath and softly curved her four fingers upward. "Four islands, out beyond the horizon, beyond where fisherman and traders and soldiers venture. He saw birds flying to and returning from there."

"And those islands could be four guano-coated hunks of rock, could they not?"

She looked away from him and seemed uncertain. Then she took a breath and faced him. "My father saw… maybe it was a vision… I mean he was so high up, so far away. Anyway, he said he saw two people there. A young man and a young woman. He saw them. I know he did, or he wouldn't have told me this." Then she picked up her pack and started up the hill that led to the ridge.

"One more thing," Chacho called. He went to the thicket and broke off two solid twigs. One he planted in the dirt by Roberto's hand. The other he tucked into Melinda's hair tie. "I believe you," he said, and they headed east.

Hours later, as darkness fell, they tucked themselves into a hollow among rocks. Chacho built a quick hot fire at the lowest point so no flames would be visible from anywhere in the surrounding countryside. Melinda scurried to put dried meat and greens into her small pot with water to make a stew. Light and shadow flickered as she worked, so much so that she looked up, wondering. There was Chacho jumping, kicking, flinging, dancing, just like the flames. She almost laughed, but his intensity reminded her of Roberto walking his fingers down his own back. So she watched quietly until he settled himself beside her, breathing hard.

It was another minute before he spoke. "I had to build the fires every evening, and the men rested and ate and were warm. But I was banished from the circle, from the comfort of the fire and had to dance to keep from shivering. They laughed at me – figured me for a fool." His face was thoughtful. Then he raised his chin and his voice. "Tonight it was a dance of freedom." He flung his head and arms skyward as though he might fly next. "Ah HA!"

At that, a thin blade of straw fell from his curly hair, straw left from his hours of hiding in the ravine. "Oh look," Melinda laughed, picking it up between two fingers. "Straw to sleep in!" And she blew it into the space between big rocks where they had cleared an area for their packs and blankets.

Their breathing slowed, and awareness of the realities of their situation returned along with their tiredness. "Collecting some grasses would be a good idea," he said, but neither of them moved.

"Never mind," she said, and she reached into the pack. She pulled out the single piece of fruit that had been in the spring house. "This is what grows on Father's and my hiding place tree." She breathed on the skin and polished it on her skirt before cutting it in half. "The birds eat most of them, and we always figured that's why their songs are so lovely." She handed him his piece, and they bit in simultaneously.

"Oh," they both sighed. Without another word, they crawled to the clear area and unrolled their blankets, not even noticing the accumulation of soft straw beneath. The last flickers of the fire translated into flickers of dreams.

Melinda was awakened by voices, but even before she opened her eyes, Chacho's hand on her arm said clearly, "Be still." She moved only her eyes and saw him absorbed in listening – listening to the language of his former masters. She, meanwhile, took in the unfathomable mysteries of the straw beneath their bodies and the dense thicket all around them. She pinched herself. She tried to lift her head but was held fast at the back of her hair. She untied the cloth strip that bound her ponytail and realized that the thicket twig Chacho had placed there had taken root overnight and grown to conceal all evidence of their presence.

The voices and footsteps didn't pause, but Chacho turned to her and put his finger to his lips. She nodded, then pointed at the straw and the thicket, and his eyebrows shot up. They listened until nothing could be heard but the morning breeze and their own breathing. Finally, indicating their hiding place, he whispered, "Is it real?" When she nodded yes, that seemed to be enough.

They rose and began to roll their blankets, and she asked what the men had said. "They are scouts looking for a way that the army can attack the highlands from a new direction. They landed a boat at the base of the cliff." And here he laughed.

"They're so angry at their leaders for sending them on such a wild goose chase. They had to make a long, long detour – nearly to the tip of the peninsula before they found a way to access the ridge. So they're running low on provisions and getting hungry. Ah." And his expression changed to one of regret. "Some highlanders will end up paying for the soldiers' displeasure, I'm afraid."

Melinda looked back in the direction of her former home. Then she turned and said with certainty, "And we will be gone."

"We will?"

"It's my father's vision." She tied her blanket to her backpack, broke off a new thicket twig and attached it to the back of her head with her hair bow. As Chacho leaned over his own pack, she inspected his curls. "You have quite a bit of straw in your hair." He raised his hand to his head, and she quickly added, "Do NOT brush it out. Come on." And she led the way out of the thicket through a single small gap between branches and boulder.

"Bossy sister," he said.

But she reached for his hand as they walked further east that day. He found water in places she would not even have thought to look and offered her the first sips, attached the heavy skin bags to his own pack. And they shared their dreams of the night before, dreams that had been pushed aside in the danger and drama of the morning, but that returned on the warm, salt-tinged air of the afternoon.

"It must have been because of the fruit," Melinda said. "My dream was filled with bird song. And safety. And peace."

"Me too." Chacho scrunched his eyes. "But isn't it strange to be able to dream of safety and peace when neither of us has ever known either one?"

"We haven't known them on the outside, maybe. But inside,

we have, I think." She searched his face. "You remembered the hand on your head."

Tears came to his eyes as he nodded. "And in my dream last night, whether it was the birds speaking or the person whose hand touched me... I don't know. I think they were saying my name."

"They were saying 'Chacho'?"

"No." He grimaced. "Chacho just means 'Kid' in their language. That's all I've been called since I was four."

Melinda stopped and faced him. "Could you hear what it was? Your name?"

"I'm... not sure." His forehead crinkled. "I think it was Daniel."

"Daniel," she said softly and squeezed his hand. "D. So maybe you are not my brother."

"Maybe not."

They walked in silence until the sun went down behind them. And there they stood at the edge of a high, sheer cliff. Far below, silver waves thumped on a sandy shore, and a gouge in the beach from the water's edge to the base of the escarpment led their eyes to the vessel.

Chacho's – Daniel's – eyes gleamed. "Yes, that's their boat." Then he laughed. "No, it's my boat! I was the one to pilot it for years as they raided seaside villages." All of a sudden, his look of satisfaction faded. "We have to reach it before they do." And he peered northward in hopes of spotting an access trail to the beach. He hadn't forgotten one word of the soldiers' complaints about their long detour.

Melinda's confidence had grown as he had despaired. "We will climb down to the boat first thing in the morning." At his incredulous sniff, she said, "Let's make camp, and I'll show you."

As they had the evening before, they found a low spot among sheltering stones. Daniel, getting used to his new old name now, demonstrated again his talent for fire-building. Melinda made the stew and cleared a sleeping area, and then they ate. He watched her expectantly.

"Well, here is my plan," she said. "But first…" And she pulled a single piece of straw out of his curls and blew it toward the cleared space. She disentangled the thicket cutting from her hair tie and planted it at the edge of their campsite near the drop-off to the sea. Then she reached toward Daniel's hair again and he, looking sheepish, reached toward hers. "Wait, not yet," she said and took his hand in her own and brushed her lips against it. "I need more straw."

She pulled three long golden segments from his hair, and he laughed with surprise, but her gaze remained serious. Her fingers worked nimbly to braid the tiny strands together. Then she poked one end of the braid into the same hole that the twig had gone into, and she closed her eyes and blew on it. It rippled and tossed and waved. "A dance of freedom," she said.

"Really?" he said without sarcasm or scorn.

"I believe so."

They leaned back against a rock and again felt the fatigue that swift change and brave action can bring. Melinda wiped out the stew pot and opened the pack to put it away. "I wish there had been more fruit in the spring house." But when she pulled her hand back out, she held, disbelieving, another of the hiding-place tree's delicious fruits. She looked from it to Daniel and back again.

"Maybe there were two?" he suggested.

She shook her head. His mouth was watering, and he bent forward to hand her the knife, then quickly pulled it back out of her reach. "Wait," he said. "Breathe on it first, like you did yesterday."

"Really?"

"I believe so."

She did. And the string of small actions – laying leaves, touching the earth, breathing or blowing, dancing, carrying straw and twigs, sharing dreams – gained all the significance of ancient rituals. They bit into their halves of the fruit, said "Oh" together, and crawled to their warm and soft straw beds. And in their dreams that night, they saw what was to come – a climb down the cliff-face holding onto a strong braided rope, drawing trees and initials in the sand, the letters M and D closest to the water line where they would be washed away at high tide. They saw Daniel courageously pointing the boat eastward, out toward the horizon, Melinda forming a heart with her fingers and blowing through it in the direction of their travel. And finally, there was the unmistakable image of the two of them climbing to the highest point on one of the islands, standing there and looking west. For one golden hour, within the dream they both dreamed, the clouds and fog lifted from the impregnable peaks beyond the country they had left behind. And they saw a man standing on the highest pass of those mountains, waving to them in joyful recognition.

MELONIA

Once upon a time not so long ago, in a small far-away village, a baby was born to a surprised and delighted middle-aged couple, Vania and Stefan. The townsfolk declared that the newborn was the most beautiful ever seen. Neighbors dropped in, on their way to here or there, to coo over her cradle, to stroke her delicate hands and feet, to exclaim upon the perfection of her features. "What's her name?" everyone asked.

"We're taking our time to consider," said Vania, bursting with pleasure and pride. "We have to give her a name that's as lovely as she is."

"Hmmph," was Stefan's only comment. He worried that so much attention and praise would attract the Evil Eye. He realized that many considered the Evil Eye to be an old-fashioned and ridiculous superstition, but the grandmother who had raised him had been sure of its signs and its remedies. So, as she would have done, he determined to ward off danger by trickery and distraction. He'd call his beautiful girl "Chunky."

"Chunky?" shrieked Vania when she overheard his tender greeting to the baby one morning as he entered the kitchen for breakfast. "Are you crazy?" She stopped stirring the porridge and shook the spoon at him. Stefan hung his head and shrugged, one of his fingers held in his daughter's firm grasp.

"With beauty like hers, she could be our ticket to prosperity and comfort in our old age. But not if people are laughing at her… and at us! Chunky, indeed! Horrible!" She shuddered, took a deep breath, then put down the spoon and reached for her husband's hand to draw him near. "Come, my dear. Help me think of a pretty name for her."

Stefan, however, was still stuck on her use of the words "prosperity" and "comfort" in reference to their child, and he mumbled them questioningly as he shuffled across the space between them. He gave her cheek a quick peck. "Prosperity and comfort? Is that what's important?" Vania ignored the question as she turned to check the thickness of the cereal on the stove.

Stefan absentmindedly reached for a slice of cantaloupe from a plate on the counter. With his first bite came a pleased smacking of the lips. "Ahh, sweet and juicy." Then he blinked. He grinned. His eyes swiveled to his wife's serious face over the steaming pot. "Just like our baby," he said. "We could call her 'Melon'."

He hooted and jumped away as she raised the spoon again, sending hot globs of oats every which way. From behind the shelter of his arms he added, "You can put 'i-a' on the end to make it sound more like a girl's name."

At that she froze and tilted her head. "Melon-ia," she whispered. "Mel-ON-ia. No, not quite. Mel-OH-nia. How melodious." She tapped her cheek and approached the cradle. She bent over it, studying her daughter, and said, "Melonia." The infant waved her arms and legs and blew a spit bubble. "Melonia is a beautiful name," she said nodding. She turned, brisk and back to business. "Now, let's eat and get you out to the fields before the day's half gone."

Stefan ate quickly, pondering. As he headed for the door, he kissed Melonia's forehead. "I love you, Chunky," he breathed by her ear.

The old routines of married life gave way to new routines of life with a child. As soon as Melonia could hold her head up in the carrying sling, and later when she could toddle on her own two feet, Stefan took her with him to the fields. Although his wife and neighbors knew him as a quiet man, he talked to his daughter all the time. He named, for her, the rocks, the animals, and the plants, pointed out their details and their changes over time. She touched and smelled and got close to everything.

She was most curious about weather. She didn't study the clouds to imagine shapes of castles and creatures in them as many children do. She wanted to know their real names, was intrigued by words like cumulus, stratus, and cirrus, wondered what the clouds indicated by their presence, what they predicted. She was thrilled by winds and storms, and there were many hot humid summer afternoons, crackling with thunder, when Vania would stomp her foot in fury as her husband and daughter raced in the door, grass-stained, dripping, mud-spattered and laughing their heads off. But she cut short her objections each time, because it was clear to anyone with eyes that Melonia's happiness, combined with plenty of fresh air, enhanced her beauty.

In the hours that father and child were outdoors, Vania developed a new passion of her own. She used some of her egg and milk money each week to purchase a length of colorful fabric. She sang happily as she sewed one-of-a-kind outfits for the girl, and every Sunday after church, she strolled through the whole town with her beautifully coifed and stylishly dressed daughter at her side. Neighbors came out to admire. "What a princess!", "What a treasure!", "How priceless!"

Stefan still had a sense of foreboding about all this fuss over his Chunky, for of course he still called her that out in the fields. Luckily, from the moment the girl could talk, she understood that the nickname was a secret between herself and her father. He didn't mention the Evil Eye. He didn't want to scare her. But in addition to calling her Chunky, he sometimes disguised her by putting a dab of mud on her nose or giving her one of his old work shirts to wear when she got chilly. He pointed out all the beauties of the world, but never mentioned her own beauty. He did all of this to protect her.

Stefan couldn't object to his wife's sewing projects and fashion parades around town on the grounds of extravagance or wastefulness, because as soon as Melonia grew out of a set of clothes (and she grew quickly – sure to be a tall girl) the items were sold to other mothers, eager to enhance the good looks of their own daughters. Vania smiled broadly as she showed her husband the money her creations had earned. "See? Our daughter attracts wealth."

Stefan shivered. "But money is such a cold thing, Wife. It is love that keeps us warm in this house." Again, she ignored his words.

When Melonia started school, Vania opened a dress shop on the village square. Her reputation as a seamstress had spread to neighboring towns and beyond, and she was always busy.

Stefan missed the girl's presence in the fields as he did morning chores. But he now took a late lunch break so he could pick her up after school. On the way home, she chattered about what she was learning. And she was proud to tell him that, whenever the teacher talked about the weather, she could add details that impressed the whole class. Then her face intensified. "But, Papa," she said, "today we learned about extreme weather – you know, tornadoes and hurricanes. Can you imagine?" So they shared what little they knew, and Melonia spent the rest of the walk home alternately twirling ferociously or running in a circle around her father. She called him the eye of the storm.

They had a few hours to wander or work, but by four forty-five, she had to be cleaned up and at her mother's shop. That was the arrangement. For every weekday, when the town clock on the tower chimed five, a wooden boy and a wooden girl emerged from opposite sides of the clock face, whirred toward each other, met in the center, leaned forward to kiss, then trundled back to where they'd started. A crowd would be gathered in the square by this time, men from their work places and women from their errands, to enjoy, not the clock which they'd seen every day of their lives, but a vision of loveliness named Melonia. The disappearance of the figurines on the tower was the cue for her breath-taking entrance into the display window of her mother's dress shop. Outfitted in Vania's latest creation, she crossed the small enclosed space, back and forth, three times – the first time as though she were a stiff wooden figure on wheels, then like a more flexible doll, a modern one whose head could turn, whose arms could swing, whose eyes could blink. On the third traverse, she was pure Melonia – a lively, healthy, confident child, a blur of movement. Just before leaving the little stage, she turned to the audience, leaned forward, and blew a kiss. The onlookers crowed and clapped, and the crowds grew larger each week.

Afterward, in the shop's small dressing room, Vania helped her daughter out of the outfit she had modeled that day and put the clothing on the mannikin that would grace the front window for most of the next day. "You are the golden girl of fashion," she told Melonia. "You are worth your weight in precious stones."

Some years later, when Melonia graduated from school, Vania, with that thought still in mind, gave her a gift of small diamond earrings. Melonia clipped them on as the three of them were getting ready to head out the door for the ceremony. The girl didn't know anyone who wore diamonds in real life, and she found herself caught up in the dazzle and sparkle of them. She stood before the hallway mirror and turned her head this way and that. When Stefan came up behind her and put his hands on her shoulders, she asked, "What do you think, Papa?"

"Well, let me see," he said and squinted at her reflection. "Actually, they remind me of how raindrops glisten on the heads of wheat in the field."

"Oh for heaven's sake," snapped Vania. "Can't you just tell your daughter she looks beautiful?" She hustled them out the door.

During the short walk to the school, Stefan couldn't help but continue his teasing. He pointed to Melonia's straight slender nose. "Here's the ridge where the cows like to graze." He indicated her eyes. "And here are the ponds where, when you were little, you always said the frogs were jumping into the sky." Gesturing toward her lips, he said, "And here's that patch of wild roses that insists on trying to take over the garden." Vania's frown made father and daughter laugh all the more.

The coming summer would see the last of Melonia's five o'clock performances and the last of her time in the fields. In the fall, she planned to attend university in the capital city to study meteorology.

Stefan struggled with the thought of her so far from home. He felt he had to squeeze out every moment he could before then. He took to standing near the door of his wife's shop every afternoon at five o'clock, but he didn't watch his daughter. He watched the faces watching her. He scowled at any hint of salaciousness. He wished more than anything to send her out into a trustworthy world.

But then one day he saw it – the Evil Eye. A young man right by the shop window followed the beauty's every move with a large black camera. Its continual clicking brought to Stefan's mind snapping jaws, sharp hooves, impatient claws – the very devil himself.

"Stop!" Stefan yelled, but no sound emerged from his lips. His hands went to his throat. Meanwhile, Melonia had blown her kiss to the crowd, and most of the onlookers were making their departures.

The photographer stood with his camera lowered, smiling in Stefan's direction. The older man lowered his arms and felt a flutter of recognition.

"Do you remember me, Sir?" the young man said, holding out his hand in greeting. "It's Tomas, your neighbor's grandson. As a boy, I spent parts of each summer here. Melonia was one of my regular play-mates."

Stefan nodded dumbly, for he did indeed remember the boy, remembered him fondly, and was struggling to mesh those feelings with the rush of fear he'd experienced seeing the camera aimed at his precious daughter. Tomas continued – something about working for a city newspaper, being here on assignment. His face broke into a huge grin as he raised his camera and tapped it with his forefinger. "These pictures of her will boost my career, for certain."

And there it was again, that glimpse into a place of madness, where people are equated with money. But then, just as quickly, Tomas was hauling him out, rescuing him. He'd pulled a photo from a pocket in his camera case and was holding it out to show him.

"This is a copy of the original. You may have it, if you'd like. It's the first good picture I ever took." It was a perfect image of Chunky – about eight years old, dirty, grass-stained, and barefoot in the field.

Stefan took it with trembling hands. "I can keep this?" He felt torn in two by the world this young man exemplified – the world that both cherished his daughter and that would pull her far from home and have its way with her. If they were two halves of the same whole, there was no way for him to protect her any longer.

When Melonia left for university at the end of the summer, Stefan tried to calm his own nerves by reminding himself that she would be studying meteorology, a fascination they'd shared for years and would, he hoped, continue to share. Vania was delighted that Tomas's photographs of their daughter had opened doors to the larger world of fashion in the city.

"She'll make such good money," she said.

"I don't want her to be distracted from her school work," he mumbled, knowing his wife wouldn't be listening to him anyway.

Melonia's letters to her parents, during the first year, were long and detailed and full of what she was learning and seeing and the people she was meeting in the course of her studies. They reminded Stefan of how she used to chatter during their walks home after school when she was young. In late spring, however, he was heart-broken to learn that his daughter wouldn't be home over the summer holidays, because she'd been offered a job in fashion modeling.

Her letters during those three busy months told of meeting photographers and agency representatives and designers. She joked that she sometimes had to act like the doll that she had impersonated in her mother's shop window. Vania chortled heartily at this, but Stefan did not. "Life in the city is quite a whirlwind," Melonia wrote. "I'm getting a storm of offers." "I thought I'd just take a few jobs, but when it rains, it pours." After a lifetime of studying weather patterns, her father could predict where this was heading.

Sure enough, Melonia left school. Vania started collecting all of the newspaper clippings, magazine ads and covers, and promo shots featuring her beautiful daughter. She kept them in a fancy box and looked through them almost every day. Stefan had framed the picture of Chunky that Tomas had given him, and it sat on the round table beside his reading chair. He didn't look at the materials in the box. To him, they didn't even resemble his daughter. They were flat. They seemed as plastic as a cheap doll. She didn't even look happy in any of the pictures. Her lips were always pouting.

Years passed, and without Melonia's youthful energy around the house, Vania and Stefan both started to feel their age. Vania's strained eyes could no longer see well enough to thread needles and do measurements, so she sold her business. Stefan's legs and back and hands were worn out from years of farm labor. He still kept chickens and grew greens and herbs in pots on the sunny side of the house, but the rest of the land was rented out.

Melonia had been sending money home since her career first took off. Stefan told her there was no need, but Vania made regular references to "a comfortable old age" as she thanked her daughter during phone calls. The young beauty's work was taking her to Milan, Paris, even New York. She sent postcards, with greetings in Italian, French or English, and followed by a hastily dashed-off impersonal line or two. They went into the box with the photos, for Vania to admire and Stefan to ignore.

Then, half a world away, on a window-rattling rain-thrashing night, Melonia's flight was cancelled due to harsh and unseasonable weather. She sat alone in a hotel room in New York City and saw *The Wizard of Oz* for the first time. She was so thrilled and terrified by the tornado scene that she lowered herself to the floor and planted her hands and feet. She was in the same situation as Dorothy – she was Dorothy. She too had been picked up, breathlessly twirled away, and thumped down in confusing places in the midst of very strange strangers. She wished she had a yellow brick road to show her the way. As it was, she could hardly put two thoughts together most days, between the whirlwind of travel, the lights flashing from all sides, the unending choreographed turns on runways, and the distracting sparkle of champagne bubbles and expensive jewelry. The babble of admiring crowds seemed more and more like wind roaring in her ears. Sometimes she felt dizzy. Sometimes she grew nauseous.

It took twenty years for Melonia's gale to finally subside. Her face and body had changed in that time. The fashion industry was demanding new looks – fresher, younger. Somewhere during that long storm-tossed season her parents had died, and although she knew she had gone to their funerals, all she could remember was a grief-filled howling inside her own head while gusts and driving rain had, both times, whipped withered bouquets around the cemetery. Surrounded by former friends and neighbors, now shy around her, she felt like a bumbling foreigner. She stuttered through phrases of the language she'd grown up with, and old memories wrapped in the words of her mother tongue became as holey and fragile as moth-eaten fabric.

Then one fine New York day, a wealthy older man with connections to the fashion industry proposed to her, and not knowing what else to do or where else to go, she said yes. By his side, there were still travels and flashing cameras and too much champagne, but the focus was more on him, and that was a relief to Melonia. During long flights or extended business meetings or media interviews or parties that were just excuses for networking, she started picking up newspapers and magazines and searching for stories about extreme weather caused by climate change. She wished she could talk to her father about it, because her husband scoffed whenever she broached the topic.

She imagined Stefan standing at the calm center of a storm. Streaks of pale blue wind swirled around him without ruffling his clothes or messing up his hair or snatching away his voice. He nodded his head as he listened to her talk about new meteorological research from the Arctic, the Antarctic, low-lying South Seas islands, and glacier-topped mountains. He asked for the human interest stories, too. He liked the ones where survivors of extreme weather events reported jerking awake, sometimes long after storms were over, to find themselves back in their own bodies. When the victims said that there came a day when they could look at the devastation around them and find the energy to start the clean-up, Stefan would breathe a sigh of relief and look at her pointedly.

For Melonia, that day of waking up coincided with the day she learned she was pregnant. She arrived home from the doctor's office and walked up to the front door of the mansion she and her husband considered their principal residence. The gardener was packing up for the day. He had just mowed the lawn, and the smell of fresh grass was rich and warm. She closed her eyes and inhaled more deeply than it seemed she had in years. After three glorious breaths, she realized that this verdant scent was her favorite in the whole world, and she decided, on the spot, to stop wearing perfumes, even the expensive ones her husband had bought for her. She breathed again into the lowest part of her abdomen, put her hand on her belly and whispered, "Okay, Chunky. Let's do it."

Then she opened her eyes, kicked off her shoes, turned, and

went back down the brick steps to the walkway. She turned left onto the soft lawn. Her toes curled with pleasure. Melonia let her hands brush bushes and flowers and stones as she meandered along the front of the house, the side of the house, the back of the house, the other side of the house. She listened to chirping and screeching and cackling birds, and there – there was the sound, from somewhere, of moving water. How had she never heard that before? She followed it to the far corner of the property, the wild corner, which she decided in that moment to claim as her own – hers and the child's.

The afternoon sun grew more golden as she continued her circuits of the property. She tilted her head back, feeling curious about the clouds, reclaiming that part of who she was, who she'd always been. She walked counter-clockwise around and around that shell of a home more than twenty times, until her feet were grass-stained and dirty.

M.E.L.

M.E.L. and V.N.F. teased anyone who had a W among their call letters. All those stupid syllables! So they taunted, "Wormy wobbly witch," or "Weird weak wastebasket."

They hardly knew what those teasing words meant. They were underworld words from a long time ago before the planet was perfected. Even adults could hardly explain. They'd say, "Wormy is something like the opposite of impermeable, and wobbly is sort of the opposite of smooth. Witches were underworld beings, so there is nothing to know." Oh well, it was fun to say them anyway. The girls shared new ones at the speed tube stop with other kids on the way to school. "Dirt," they'd snicker. "Bacteria," they'd snort.

Call letters and the creativity of the teasing they inspired helped to establish the Essential Pecking Order. But they were also important as connectors between friends. When V.N.F. said Merry Energetic Lady or Most Evanescent Light, and when M.E.L. replied with Very Nice Forget-Me-Not or Vivacious Neat Friend, the bonds between them were strengthened and the time they shared became more perfect.

They lived on P.P.A., Perfect Planet A. It was the original perfect planet, and the girls were taught in school that it was the best, because it was where life began. Planets B and C had been established, and D was under construction but required more atmospheric and hydrospheric support than P.P.A. The girls sometimes talked about their X, Y and Z call letter siblings and wondered which perfect planet, B or C, they lived on. Those bio-pairings were always shipped away because by the time the twenty-fourth, twenty-fifth and twenty-sixth children were grown from, in M.E.L.'s case, eggs from a biological egg donor whose first call letter was M, there was occasionally some protein breakdown or chromosomal damage which led to less than perfect children, unsuitable for the A planet.

Much as M.E.L. loved her friend V.N.F., she wondered about her creation. V.N.F. did not score high on the intelligence scale. The F at the end of her call letters indicated she was only the sixth V bio-pairing. But maybe one or both of her parents had had a V or W as their third call letter. To make sure her mental slowness did not result in a pecking order drop, V.N.F. had honed her teasing skills. Sometimes what she said was hurtful. She suggested that Ws should be relocated along with Xs, Ys and Zs, because their names were too much trouble to say.

After spending four hours each day at individual task terminals at school with breaks for nutrition intake, breath work, and exercise periods, children had two hours of free time before they were required to report to their First Letter houses. Thus M children, like M.E.L., lived in a house staffed by M mothers. All children wishfully, and privately, claimed one of the mothers as their biological egg donor. M.E.L.'s favorite was M.L.P., whose call letters, she whispered to herself, stood for My Loving Parent. M.E.L. had not met an E father, either at school or on recreational outings, whom she cared to think of as her possible sperm donor.

M.E.L. felt lucky to have V.N.F. for company in her free hours after school. They liked to do the same things, and neither of them signed up for sports or arts. Sometimes they swam in the big artificial lake, but their favorite place to go was the slide slope. The smooth polymer surface of P.P.A. had been slightly mounded at designated recreation locations, and fifteen steps took one to the highest point. There, one could run for five meters before meeting the slope, which had been treated with a traction-less coating. What joy, thought M.E.L. to test the edge of control!

Control was the highest value in P.P. culture. That's why the peaks and valleys of the underworld had been covered and filled in with perfect plastic and why, beneath the carefully designed and uncluttered surface, were hidden the vast air and water filtration systems, the essential supplies construction zones, and the nutrient manufacturing plants. That's also why egg donors and sperm donors were paired scientifically ensuring the viability and variability of the gene pool. That's why clothing and foot coverings were standardized and could be traded for new sizes to account for growth in young people and weight redistribution in adults.

Clothing and foot coverings were only removed in the evening for sanitation procedures after which one walked directly to one's sleeping berth. M.E.L. had never heard anyone comment on the sensation of that short barefoot walk. But every night, M.E.L. lay awake listening to the breathing of other M children shift into sleep mode while she savored the tingling aliveness of the soles of her feet.

One day, when M.E.L. and V.N.F. were playing on the slide slope, M.E.L. took off her foot coverings and said, "V.N.F., watch this!" She ran the few steps and launched herself onto the traction-less surface. Her arms flailed and she fought for balance as she sped down the mound and glided twice as far as she ever had before. She expected to hear V.N.F. cheer, but her friend was staring at her with horror.

"M.E.L., get up here," she hissed. "Do you want people to call you Mixed-up Eccentric Loony?" She turned her back on her playmate until she heard M.E.L.'s foot coverings snap back around her ankles. V.N.F. faced her with a twisted scowl. "What on P.P.A. made you do that?"

M.E.L. looked down at her feet. "I don't know. I didn't think." She shrugged. "It was more like my feet made me." V.N.F. was already stomping down the steps when M.E.L. added in a whisper, "It was fun."

The incident wasn't mentioned again, but M.E.L. realized that her friend didn't address her with heart-warming call letter creations any more. She noticed that V.N.F. cast suspicious glances her way as they walked and played. M.E.L. was surprised at the lack of hurt she felt. In fact, some days, she could hardly wait to get away from her friend a few minutes early. When she was out of sight of V.N.F. and others, she scurried off the trail that led to M house, took off her foot coverings and ran among the silk and silicone trees. At first, she was scared she might be spotted. The teasing would be terrible. She could just hear it, "Mutinous Evil Lay-about" and "Monstrous Egotistical Loser." But she soon realized that nobody else ever left the designated pathways. This somehow made her so happy she wished H was one of her call letters.

She found the off-areas very calming. Things were not as linear. Shadows crossed and criss-crossed at odd angles. Fallen imperfect foliage bits littered the ground. M.E.L. loved to step on them, discovering the sensation of not-perfect through her feet.

She cut shorter and shorter her time after school with V.N.F. She said she hadn't slept well and needed a rest period or that her stomach had been upset at nutrition intake time and now she was hungry. V.N.F. said, "Oh, E is for Excuses, I see." And stamped off.

M.E.L. walked farther and farther from designated trails on

her uncovered feet but kept an eye on her wrist computer for compass bearings and the time. One could not be late for afternoon arrival at First Letter Houses. All children had nightmares about unknown forces that could prevent a timely return. It wasn't potential consequences that made those dreams so frightening. It was the possibility of beyond-controlness, an evil so dark it was never discussed, infinitely worse than witches and other underworld imperfections.

So M.E.L. triangulated her position and figured her return times with precision. She made sure to put on her foot coverings and step back onto the main trail out of sight of M House. It would arouse suspicion if she appeared from a non-usual direction.

But one day, she didn't look at her wrist calculator, didn't do her time and distance calculations. She'd seen a shimmering in the silk trees ahead and had run toward it as toward a long-awaited gift. She stood at the edge of a grove where leaves fluttered bronze in the late afternoon light. Usually foliage movement was only seen in the proximity of ventilators from under-surface heating and cooling units. M.E.L.'s learning materials had referred to this air movement as wind, but that just seemed like another meaningless W word.

M.E.L. looked carefully before proceeding. There were no ventilation units in sight, so she stepped hesitantly among the trees. Immediately her gaze went to her bare feet. She wiggled her toes then dropped and placed her hands on the polymer surface. It was warm, and from this angle she could see waves of air rising slowly, prodding the undersides of leaves, telling a secret.

M.E.L. crawled to the middle of the grove and stretched out on her back. She had never felt such perfect warmth, not even in her sleeping berth at night. Never had she had a dream as lovely as the dance of light and matter above her.

Later she woke in the dark and realized, within seconds, that she was so far outside the boundaries of the Perfection Proscriptions that she had no idea how to return to the life she'd lived for the thirteen years since her creation. There were no rules or guidelines about atoning for such mistakes, because mistakes of this magnitude were not conceivable.

M.E.L. scrambled up from the warm surface, checked her bearings and raced out of the grove. She stopped to put on her foot coverings as though that would make her crime less. Then she set a course directly for M House knowing that, in the dark, her approach would not be seen.

No one went out at night. She was seeing the moon for the first time without having to press her hands to the sides of her face and then against the glass to block interior reflections. Its light was cooler than she thought it would be. Moon shadows were sharper, bluer, denser than day shadows. She sniffed the night air – different than day air – more tickly. Her senses wanted to linger over this forbidden feast.

But suddenly, she found herself before M House and saw the dormitory windows dark. The only light came from the Mothers' Lounge on the first floor. M.E.L. approached and peered in.

The only mother there was M.L.P., the one M.E.L. had chosen as her desired egg donor because she smiled often and her eyes moved more than those of other mothers. Sometimes, she even touched.

The mother reached to shut down her entertainment unit and rose to leave the lounge. M.E.L. held her breath and tapped on the window. M.L.P. looked around startled. M.E.L. tapped again and put her face close to the glass.

The mother's face looked frightened, and she pressed a hand to her chest. M.E.L. could read her lips – "What on P.P.A.? What on P.P.A.?" she was saying. They stared at each other for minutes before the mother was able to move.

Finally she came to the window, deactivated the emergency sensors and pressed the opening device. She seemed unsure of her actions, nervous in case an alarm should sound. But the quiet remained unbroken, and the mother held out a trembling hand which M.E.L. grabbed and spontaneously kissed. She pulled herself up and through the narrow opening. M.L.P. reversed the activation procedures and without looking at M.E.L., rubbed the back of her hand against her uniform. She said, "I will escort you to the sick room."

She pointed M.E.L. to a pure white sleeping berth. The girl perched there and held herself as though she might otherwise explode. She watched as the mother logged in "M.E.L. five p.m. Mild sedative to dispel upset and confusion. No further treatment deemed necessary at…" and she checked her wrist computer "…eleven forty-five p.m." She handed M.E.L. a yellow tablet to suck on, pointed to the log-in notes, said, "That's what happened." Then left the room. M.E.L. lay back stiffly, worked the tablet with her tongue, and by the time it had dissolved, she was asleep.

Because the yellow pills resulted in ten hours of uninterruptable sleep, M.E.L. woke the next morning already over an hour late for school. M.L.P. entered the sick room and said, "You will go to school, and there will be consequences." She did not smile or touch. Her eyes were hard.

M.E.L. trudged the trail and took the speed tube alone. She could hear her pulse in her ears. It was nutrition intake time when she crossed the building's threshold, and she saw V.N.F. with a group of gossiping girls, leaning in avidly. She walked the aisle to the nutrition portion storage unit and heard whispers of, "Mysteriously Eerily Late," and "Muddy Eely Lazybones." She pulled out a nutrition package and held it in view of her classmates, but as she turned, her other hand slipped a second package into her pocket.

From that time on, the whispers never ceased. M.E.L. figured that V.N.F. had told everyone about her early departures from the recreation area. Other M children could accurately report that she was rarely seen along the designated trail, or at M House, until minutes before arrival time. V.N.F.'s teasing was the worst. She creatively combined M.E.L.'s call letters for a new kind of taunt. The children's laughter was screechy when V.N.F. shouted, "Mel-ignant, Mel-evolent, Mel-odorous!"

M.E.L. started moving her clothing and toiletries from the personal storage locker at the foot of her sleeping berth and hiding them in her pillowcase or under corners of her mattress. At every opportunity, she tucked supplementary nutrition packages into her pockets and, at the end of each day, placed them layer upon layer into the trunk. When she had kitchen duty between arrival time and the evening meal, she stole sharp or abrasive objects, although children were not permitted to touch such implements. She slid them along the front edge of her locker box. Each night, as she trod the short and straight pathway from the sanitation station to her sleeping berth, she imagined those few sweet barefoot steps taking her closer and closer to the warm grove of fluttering trees.

The day came when her storage trunk was full of food and tools. She woke early and rubbed her face, ears and collarbone until they were red and hot. When morning chimes sounded, instead of rising with the others, she curled into a tense ball. The mother on duty found her thus, helped her into her clothes, escorted her to the sick room and said she'd be back once the others had departed for school. M.E.L. rubbed her head and neck even harder, pressed her fist into her stomach to remind herself to stay slouched.

When the mother returned, she logged in, noted her observations and listed treatments – a poultice for irritated skin and feverishness and a yellow sedative tablet for general upset and stomach ache. "In ten hours' time, you should be fine," the mother said, placing the poultice on M.E.L.'s forehead and the tablet on her tongue.

As soon as the mother turned her back, M.E.L. flicked the yellow pill from her mouth. When the door had closed behind her, the girl jumped up, laid two pillows lengthwise under the white blanket and placed the poultice at the top end of the mound. She slid open the supplies cupboard and grabbed the largest bag of hydration capsules. Then, hardly breathing, she released the door mechanism and listened at the opening until all sounds of staff members heading to their quarters, to task centers, or to the lounge had ceased.

M.E.L. crept silently through deserted corridors. Back in the dormitory, she activated the air casters on her storage trunk and guided it to the main entryway, guaranteed to be deserted at this time of day.

As she exited the building, she whispered, "M.E.L. logging out." And she didn't look back. Even if one of the mothers should see her, M.E.L. now understood there would be no action taken. There were no guidelines for counteracting such blatant imperfection unless… and it occurred to M.E.L. that this might be the purpose of the new D planet.

She strode into the silk and silicone forest that surrounded

M House. When she reached the warm grove of chattering trees, she spoke firmly. "I am M.E.L. which stands for My Experimental Life." The leaves applauded and she bowed.

She deactivated the air casters on her trunk and took out the tools she had stolen from the kitchen. She chose a spot within a cluster of five trees as her digging site. The sharpest knife was needed to cut through the impermeable, opposite of wormy, surface layer, but once M.E.L. had peeled aside a sleeping berth-sized rectangle of the planet's plastic hide, the material below was more spongy and scoopable.

She worked through the day until her arms shook with fatigue and she had enough room for her storage box and herself under-surface. She ate, swallowed a hydration capsule and lay on her back in her warm nest, looking up at the sky. She made up names for the stars, like Simple Shining Spark and Only Orange Orb until she fell asleep.

In the coming days, M.E.L. continued to cut away at the flesh of P.P.A., creating a diagonally descending tunnel. She removed each day's scraps and chunks to the cavities where she had tucked her trunk, or her tired self, the night before. At one point, she realized the warmth she associated with the grove was becoming an intense heat, emanating from somewhere to her right. She could see a distant red glow through the polymer. "The underworld has fire," she said to herself in awe. So she angled her tunnel to the left and dug deeper.

Her hands and arms grew muscled, and she could tell she was making greater progress as time went on. Progress toward what she could not say. Sometimes she imagined herself emerging through the surface on the opposite side of P.P.A. More often, she assumed she would come to the underworld. But although she knew underworld teasing words like garbage can and slug, she didn't know what those things might look like, didn't know if she should be afraid.

Then one day, the filtered light and the blue-silver hue of her tunneled surroundings changed. She saw darker colors below and a scritchy-scratchy texture unlike anything perfectly manufactured. She had to get the sharp knife back out of her trunk to cut through another impermeable layer. And there it was. "Dirt," she said without knowing how she knew.

The light in the few feet of space between the polymer and the surface of the underworld was like what she'd experienced while swimming underwater in the artificial lake. The plastic ceiling paralleled the contours of the ground and reminded her of the waves she'd splashed in. M.E.L. wriggled with excitement and said, "Wormy," as she drew curved lines with her fingers in the dry soil.

Then she heard a sound that, with its dancing rhythms, reminded her of the silk leaves above in the warm grove. She scuttled toward it as eagerly and fearlessly as she had first approached the quivering trees. It was a spring, bubbling up through a bowl of stones. And then water sprang also from her eyes and dripped from her nose and jaw into the pool as she considered this wonder. She lowered her head and drank and drank.

The surface of the underworld was cooler than the polymer above, and M.E.L. started to shiver. She cut an opening in the impermeable ceiling over her head and peeled it back as she had done on P.P.A.'s surface so long, it seemed, ago. She carved out an overhead sleeping berth and, in this way, also had extra space in which to sit and stand and stretch. She decided to leave her storage unit at the base of the tunnel, sitting on the underworld's surface. No, she told herself. She would no longer call it underworld, with all of that word's nasty associations. From now on, she would just call it world.

When she woke the next morning, she felt cramping in her gut and wondered if the liquid hydration had made her ill after the weeks of taking hydration tablets. Then she noticed stickiness between her legs and saw blood and realized, with a start, that her life on P.P.A. would have totally changed on this very day. She would have been moved out of M House, handed a school graduation certificate and, for the next twenty-six years, been an egg donor and an invisible worker below-surface. She and V.N.F. had spoken of this day with dread. Today, in her new home, she saw her body as creative and powerful and reveled in the possibilities.

She thought her eggs might be in the blood so she squatted on the world and mixed her flow with the dirt to plant some new life. She transferred the remaining hydration tablets into one of her foot coverings with the top folded over and tied. Then she filled the large tablet bag with water so that, away from the spring, she could clean the stickiness and grittiness from her skin. She enjoyed the squishy feeling of the mud she'd made and had to wash again.

Five days later the bleeding stopped, and M.E.L. set out on hands and knees to explore. She found spring after spring along the base of what seemed like a never-ending sliding slope – a slope she pictured as topped with fire. The springs were different temperatures and had different smells, and in one she discovered delicate green leaves, not of silk or silicone. Her thumbnail squeezed right through the tender stem of one, and she smelled it and placed it in her mouth. It was the best thing she'd ever tasted.

She returned to her storage unit each evening, until she felt ready to move farther from her tunnel. Because the trunk stood too high to maneuver through the narrow space above the world's surface, she used one of her tools to pry apart the hinges and lifted off the lid. She laid it upside-down on the dirt and placed what remained of her belongings and supplies into it. She put on her second foot covering and tied the laces to its latch so she could pull her things behind her as she crawled. She left her wrist calculator in the locker box. Now she could find her way by following the edge of the huge slide slope and the sound of water in the springs and her own tracks in the dirt – how beautiful they were! Nothing so perfect existed on the surface of P.P.A., she thought.

M.E.L. carved out overhead sleeping berths near springs as she journeyed, and when she bled each month, she mixed her blood into the soil. She lay down tired each night and admired the wonders on the ground below her and named what she saw – Red Rough Rock, Violet Vital Vein, Glittering Glassy Grains. They became her new friends. During her waking hours, she ate more leaves and fewer nutrition packages.

But then one day, she detected wavelets crossing the face of a newly discovered pool and sensed the air movement which created them. She had felt no upset since the morning she'd exited M House, but here it was again as if the wind, a W word, was teasing and provoking her.

She tore off her clothes and submerged herself in the pool to get away from its malicious whispering. She held her breath and watched the ripples slip sideways above her. Their smooth motion reminded her of her own joyous slipping, on the edge of control, down the sliding slope during her afternoons with V.N.F. That edge was a place where she excelled, where she never fell. It was how she had known she could live My Experimental Life. She wouldn't let herself listen to fear's taunts.

So when she had dressed and used her fingers to untangle her hair, much longer than it had ever been before, she moved into the wind. Soon she came upon, as she had known was inevitable, air intake and exhaust vents that fitted precisely into the space between the world and the lower impermeable surface. Flaps of black polymer hung between the vents, sections just wide enough for her to squeeze through. She lay with an eye and an ear to the edge of a flap long enough that her neck ached and one arm fell asleep. She saw no change of light levels, no signs of movement, heard no sounds of work. She crawled through and stood up.

Here was a different kind of underworld, full of ducts and gauges, large storage units and computer screens and, to her right, a staff lounge like the one in M House. All of the floors were coated so that workers who came down here to monitor and maintain the invisible workings of P.P.A. had no view of, or contact with, the underworld she'd come to know.

M.E.L. searched the storage areas in the staff lounge until she found cases of nutrition packages. She lifted two of them off a shelf and returned to the flap she'd come through. She shoved the food boxes to the other side of the membrane.

The passageway in the opposite direction ended at a tall ladder beside an elevator. Use of the elevator would most likely be detectable, she thought. So she looked way up the ladder and fought the urge to turn back, to stay safe. But she desired, so suddenly, so forcefully, to see the sky. And for the first time since she'd left her wrist computer behind, she was curious about her location on P.P.A. She climbed the countless rungs and pressed the door activator at the top.

She stepped onto the clean, flat, impermeable surface, into a night glorious with stars. The door closed behind her with a whoosh. Her breath caught when she saw that where the doorway had been there was now only seamless polymer. She searched for an external activator but found nothing. So she memorized her location in relation to the ventilation unit and tried to imagine how one might steal a worker's remote control device.

The ventilator, she saw, served a dormitory much like the one she'd lived in for thirteen years. Staying within the darkness of moon shadows, she approached the front entrance. W House, the sign read. She knew where she was – across the large artificial lake from M House. The way would be long, but she could make her way back to her tunnel over-surface. She figured the coordinates in her mind and suppressed any thoughts and fears of being seen, being reported, being prevented from returning to her world, or being sent to the D planet.

Then she heard a sound like the bubbling of a spring only sad, and she peered among the trees bordering the designated pathway to W House. There sat a boy, head drooped on his knees, foot coverings beside him. His shoulders shook, and his fists pounded perfect plastic.

M.E.L. spoke softly so as not to startle him. "It's all right." But he jumped and scuttled backward. She stepped into a patch of moonlight so he could see her better and pointed at her bare feet. "Look," she said. "You will be all right. I'll show you."

She took his hand and asked his call letters. "W.W.B.," he said as he rose, tucking his foot coverings under one arm. She introduced herself and, with the gentlest of invitations, convinced him to walk with her around the artificial lake, behind M House, and through the silk and silicone forest. She could feel him relax more and more as they journeyed through the night.

The moon set as they reached the warm grove, and the boy gasped, just as she once had, at the sensation in his feet. They sat facing each other under the waving canopy, and the boy spoke for the first time all night. He told M.E.L. he couldn't stand the teasing any more, that being a W was the worst witchy waste, that tonight he'd been locked out after arrival time, and that he couldn't go back – for all these reasons and more. There was also the matter of his love for removing his foot coverings and wandering off designated pathways.

M.E.L. lay back and patted the warm surface beside her. When he'd settled there, she told him the story of finding this grove and of returning to it with provisions. She pointed up at the stars she had named and said that when light came in the morning, she would show him an incredible and beautiful W. She called him Wonderful World Boy.

Hours later, the sun touched their faces, waking them, and M.E.L. beckoned W.W.B. to the cluster of five trees that hid the entrance to the tunnel. The foliage seemed thicker than before, and she was, at first, frightened that her hole had been discovered, sealed up and disguised with more silk trees. Then she cried out and her hands flew to her mouth. W.W.B. studied her expression, his own face tight and frowning, and he feared the worst.

She approached the stems and green leaves emerging from the tunnel, touched them, smelled them, and trembled from head to foot. "These are growing things from the world," she whispered, and W.W.B. touched them too. They discovered round fruits among the leaves that, when twisted, fell ripe and juicy into their hands. They ate until they were full.

"Come," said M.E.L. "There is so much more to see." She led the way into the downward sloping tunnel, and they hadn't gone far when, suddenly, W.W.B. said, "Wait." She turned to see him staring intently at the long vine snaking upward beside them. At first she saw nothing remarkable but then detected a slight prickle of movement, like what she saw behind her eyelids when she was dizzy from spinning fast down the slide slope. He looked at her round-eyed and smiling. "Bugs," he said, although he didn't know how he knew.

MELVIN

Melvin grew up on the prairies, which some folks might say is a curse. But when he was seventeen, he found its gift, a secret gift, the kind you don't blab about.

He was different enough anyway without going around talking about secret gifts and sounding like a stoner. It had always been awkward being Melvin Belvedere, the son of a librarian and a banker, towered over and out-bulked by big Scandinavian-stock farm kids. They were blond and tawny like the wide fields they worked, as good-natured as the animals they herded. He was brown-haired, pale, and skittish. Their eyes were blue and clear like the prairie sky. His were dark and deep like the bottom of a well. They tumbled off the school bus or out of pick-up trucks on weekday mornings. Melvin was a town kid and walked to school.

Nobody picked on him though, because he was crazy-smart and could play a mean guitar. He played for school dances and country dances and even made the national anthem, before every sports event, sound like a heavy-metal masterpiece.

His mom had taught him piano from the time he could first reach the keys until he was ten, at which point he'd asked for an electric guitar for Christmas. He taught himself how to play, said the math of it made total sense to him.

So the big hulking boys tousled Melvin's spiky hair when they passed him in the halls and gave him the benefit of the doubt in gym class by pretending he was invisible when he goofed up.

But that changed the day the Johannsen boys discovered him

on the grassy knoll at the back of their family's spread where it bordered the Belvedere's yard.

Melvin had first started going up there, as only a prairie kid could think of as "up there," when he was twelve and beginning to experience what his parents called the preteen blues. They were pretty cool about it and didn't say stupid stuff like "You'll grow out of it." They just encouraged him to play guitar (his mom introduced him to twelve-bar blues phrasing), write songs and take walks.

He was okay with the music parts of their advice, but take walks? A kid who walks to school every day expose himself to public view doing the same retarded thing on his own time?

So when his mom or dad saw him sulking around the house and ordered him outside, he didn't go far. He ducked around the back of the hedge that marked the border of their yard, through the fence, and up onto the knoll. He'd watch the sun set or count the cars going by on Route fourteen or run up and down the steepest part of the slope pretending he was Rocky in training.

It must have done him some good, he had to admit, because he was still going up there at age seventeen, but now more to ponder life's mysteries and his place in them. One hot May afternoon, heavy-headed and slow, he lay down on his back in the tall grass. It was some moments before he realized that the strange sensation he was feeling was the breathing and pulse of the Earth.

"Holy!" he bellowed, bolting upright. He gulped air, looking at the ground around him – nothing to see but grasses nodding their heads. He pressed his fingertips to the sides of his neck, then his palms to his chest, thinking it must have been his own heartbeat and respiration he'd picked up on. But the tempos didn't match at all. Tentatively, he lowered himself again, first to his elbows, then to his back. There it was, like a huge drum, like the whisper of a distant flute, like the lowest notes on a bass guitar, the ones you feel in your bones more than hear.

He listened to the song of it then, closed his eyes and pressed himself against the ground, believed for a small space of time that he was back in the womb, waiting to be born. The breeze picked up, and the waving grasses were the waters breaking, and he took huge gasping breaths and realized that he had an enormous aching hard-on.

That's when the Johannsen brothers, out checking their fence line, topped the rise and saw Melvin with the front of his shorts jutting skyward.

"What the hell, Mel?" they roared, doubling up with laughter. Melvin pressed his hands to his crotch, tried to pretend he'd been asleep, tried to laugh with them. But there it stood, irrefutable evidence of something geeky going on, and Melvin couldn't stammer out one word.

One of the brothers jeered, "Geez, you could fly a flag on that!"

Melvin bolted for home, while behind him, they called, "What the hell, Mel?" over and over again.

And it didn't end there. During the final weeks of the school year, all the kids started snickering, "What the hell, Mel?" As they passed him in the halls, in the gym, in the bathrooms. And one morning as he approached school on foot, the Johannsens and some of their buddies, getting off the bus, grinned and pointed from Melvin to the custodian coming out the side door of the school to raise the provincial and national flags.

One of them shouted, "Hey, Mel, what flag are you hoisting today?" Melvin stopped in his tracks, felt his whole body go hot, and turned as though tempted to run home again. But the crazy-smart part of him was suddenly struck by an idea so brilliant, he jumped up in the air and landed with a whoop.

He waved as he ran past them toward the school's front door. "Thanks! Thanks! This'll be great!" He gloried in their looks of bewilderment. He made a beeline for the music room and signed out the bass guitar, asking to keep it until July second. His treble guitar wouldn't do the trick.

He took the instrument home that afternoon, tuned it as low as it could go and experimented with different objects and materials that could be used to depress or strum strings. He wanted to approximate the deep Earth sounds he'd heard on the knoll.

That evening, while his parents talked on the back deck, he set up his amp on the front porch. "Don't break any sound barriers," his mom called through the rear screen door, her way of reminding him to be respectful of neighbors.

"No worries," he said, then followed an impulse to swing out the back door and give his parents each a quick hug. Their pleased chuckles carried him, grinning, to the front of the house where he plugged in the bass and took a big breath. He turned to watch the last rays of the sun sink beneath the horizon.

Then he settled on the edge of the porch swing, held the guitar at the ready, and arranged his modified capos and picks on the seat beside him. He closed his eyes, felt his heart soften, and sent the first notes out into the purple twilight.

All became still. The crickets ceased their chirruping. Neighborhood TVs and stereos became muted. Dogs didn't bark. His mom's and dad's conversation paused. Melvin could almost see the waves of sound he was creating travel on the silent sea of deepening darkness.

And as he'd barely dared to hope, a few headlights started to appear, some taking the exit off Route fourteen, some coming from town. He kept playing. Six small cars pulled up in front of his house, and kids with instruments climbed out. A few, carrying guitar cases, he recognized as the quietest, mousiest members of pick-up bands he'd played with. A brother and sister from the reservation brought large skin drums. A hippie chick from a rival school came with her flute. One guy had a music case full of odd percussion instruments and wind chimes. Yep, the geeks, the stoners, the outsiders, thought Melvin fondly. Without a word, each set up and joined in. The sounds were sparse, gentle, full of listening, full of life.

Once the final chord had drifted away (was it minutes or hours later?) the sounds of conversation, crickets, dogs, TVs and stereos returned. The musicians huddled close, and Melvin told them about what he had heard and felt on the knoll, and of course they already knew – that's why they had come. Then he told them about the July first, Canada Day gig.

It was a tradition. The sports field behind Melvin's school was the place for Canada Day picnics, face-painting, entertainment, games and fireworks every year. Ever since he was eleven, Melvin had played his heavy-metal "O Canada" as the final fireworks lit up the sky overhead and the Maple Leaf flag was raised to the top of the flag pole. It was a celebration of community, of shared values. Melvin, not one for joining in festivities, had always cruised the edges of the action until it was time for him to play his guitar. As he thought about it now, he wasn't sure he'd ever seen any of his current band mates there. They assured him they'd be there this time.

No one even considered a need to rehearse again before July first – that would be like rehearsing how to sleep or eat – but on Canada Day, they all emerged, instruments in hand, from the edges of the crowd and met at the base of the flag pole. They set up their equipment as the sun was going down. Families spread blankets or arranged lawn chairs for optimal fireworks viewing.

The Master of Ceremonies saw that Melvin had company this year and did a quick check with him about introductions. The young musicians stood quietly, which some might have figured for professionalism. But in actuality, they were all tuning in to the music beneath their feet, letting it affect their heartbeats, their breathing.

"And now, ladies and gentlemen, boys and girls," the MC's voice came over the loudspeaker, "please rise for our national anthem, and put your hands together for Melvin and the Earthlings!"

The crowd stood and clapped and guffawed. A few voices squealed or bellowed, "Melvin and the Earthlings?" Melvin looked over the heads of all the people and answered with a complex mind-bending chord, then riffed it and reverbed it until he could feel the audience practically standing on tiptoe in anticipation. Then he played "O Canada", almost the same way he'd played it in years past. But he and the band somehow stressed the notes that went with the words "home" and "land" and "love" and "hearts" and "free". The flag went up, the fireworks flew, and as colored sparks fell and the last word was sung, there was not a dry eye in the crowd.

The final note of the bass guitar did not fade though. Melvin segued into the deep earth sounds he had played that evening on his porch. Then, gentle harmonies from the other guitars wrapped around, deep resonant drumming connected and rooted, the flute whispered long-held secrets, chimes and rattles sparked energy across synapses.

The band members felt their gaze drawn upward, and there

at the top of the flag pole, above the listless red and white Canadian flag, was a silken blue Earth flag dancing like a living thing to the music they played.

The final chord drifted away (was it minutes or hours later?). Everyone but Melvin and the Earthlings opened their eyes to find themselves catching their breaths, men and women flat on their backs in the grass with either enormous hard-ons or hands pressed against wombs, and children curled on their sides, in fetal position, thumbs in mouths. They blinked, sat up slowly, helped each other to stand. Then neighbors offered each other rides home because, they all agreed, it was silly and wasteful to have so many vehicles on the road.

In the days and weeks that followed, Melvin's mom reported that every book and magazine in the library that dealt with ecology, the environment and clean technologies had been poured over, photocopied, or checked out. At the car dealerships, lots of pick-up trucks had been traded in for electric cars, and the town council scurried to get charging stations installed. Solar panels and wind generators were shipped to, and set up at, almost every address. Farmers stopped spraying herbicides and pesticides as a first step to becoming certified organic. The custodian at the school raised the Earth flag every day, even on weekends and holidays. Curious folks from neighboring towns were driving over on Sundays to see what the buzz was all about.

The band still got together every once in a while when the sunset and the night sky were just right. Melvin, sitting on his front porch after classes at the local college or his part-time job, played a few notes on the bass guitar that his high school music teacher had insisted he keep on the condition that he continue playing that music, whatever it was. Once his friends arrived, by bicycle or skateboard or on horseback, they all walked around behind the hedge, climbed through the fence and went up on the knoll. There, they lay in the grass, under the stars and the flash of passing satellites, and listened to Earth's music, felt it in their bones. It informed their lives. It told the future.